# MY HAIRIEST ADVENTURE

## Look for more Goosebumps books by R.L. Stine:

# Goosebumps

## MY HAIRIEST ADVENTURE

### R.L. STINE

AN
**APPLE**
PAPERBACK

SCHOLASTIC INC.
New York Toronto London Auckland Sydney

A PARACHUTE PRESS BOOK

No part of this publication may be reproduced in whole or in part, or stored in a retrieval system, or transmitted in any form or by any means, electronic, mechanical, photocopying, recording, or otherwise, without written permission of the publisher. For information regarding permission, write to Scholastic Inc., 555 Broadway, New York, NY 10012.

ISBN 0-590-48350-1

Copyright © 1994 by Parachute Press, Inc. All rights reserved. Published by Scholastic Inc. APPLE PAPERBACKS is a registered trademark of Scholastic Inc. GOOSEBUMPS is a trademark of Parachute Press, Inc.

12 11 10                                                                    5 6 7 8 9/9

Printed in the U.S.A.                                                       40

First Scholastic printing, December 1994

# 1

Why were there so many stray dogs in my town?

And why did they always choose *me* to chase?

Did they wait quietly in the woods, watching people go by? Then did they whisper to each other, "See that blond kid? That's Larry Boyd — let's go get him"?

I ran as fast as I could. But it's so hard to run when you're carrying a guitar case. It kept banging against my leg.

And I kept slipping in the snow.

The dogs were catching up. They were howling and barking, trying to scare me to death.

Well, it's working, guys! I thought. I'm scared. I'm plenty scared!

Dogs are supposed to sense when you're afraid of them. But I'm not usually afraid of dogs. In fact, I really like dogs.

I'm only afraid of dogs when there's a pack of them, running furiously after me, drooling hungrily, eager to tear me to tiny shreds. Like now.

Scrambling over the snow, I nearly toppled into a drift up to my knees. I glanced back. The dogs were gaining on me.

It isn't fair! I thought bitterly. They have four legs, and I only have two!

The big black dog with the evil black eyes was leading the pack, as usual. He had his lips pulled back in an angry snarl. He was close enough so that I could see his sharp, pointy teeth.

"Go home! Go home! Bad dogs! Go home!"

Why was I yelling at them? They didn't even *have* homes!

"Go home! Go home!"

My boots slipped in the snow, and the weight of my guitar case nearly pulled me over. Somehow I staggered forward, caught my balance, and kept moving.

My heart was pounding like crazy. And I felt as if I were burning up, even though it was about twelve degrees.

I squinted against the bright glare of the snow. I struggled to run faster, but my leg muscles were starting to cramp.

I don't stand a chance! I realized.

"Ow!" The heavy guitar case bounced against my side.

I glanced back. The dogs were leaping excitedly, making wide crisscrosses across the yards, howling and yowling, as they scrambled after me.

Moving closer. And closer.

"Go home! Bad dogs! Bad! Go home!"

Why me?

I'm a nice guy. Really. Ask anybody. They'll tell you — Larry Boyd is the nicest twelve-year-old kid in town!

So why did they always chase *me*?

The last time, I dived into a parked car and shut the door just as they pounced. But today, the dogs were too close. And the cars along the street were all snow-covered. By the time I got a car door open, the dogs would be having me for dessert!

I was only half a block from Lily's house. I could see it on the corner across the street. It was my only chance.

If I could get to Lily's house, I could —

"NOOOOOOOO!"

I slipped on a small rock, hidden under the snow. The guitar case flew from my hand and hit the snow with a soft *thud*.

I was down. Facedown in the snow.

"They've got me this time," I moaned. "They've got me."

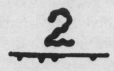

Everything went white.

I struggled to my knees, frantically brushing snow off my face with both hands.

The dogs barked hungrily.

"Scat! Get away! Get going!" Another voice. A familiar voice. "Get going, dogs! Get away!"

The barking grew softer.

I brushed the wet snow from my eyes. "Lily!" I cried happily. "How did *you* get here?"

She swung a heavy snow shovel in the dogs' direction. "Scat! Go away! Go!"

The growls turned to low whimpers. The dogs backed up, started to retreat. The huge black dog with the black eyes lowered his head and loped slowly away. The others followed.

"Lily — they're *listening* to you!" I cried thankfully. I climbed slowly to my feet and brushed the snow off the front of my blue down parka.

"Of course," she replied, grinning. "I'm tough, Larry. I'm real tough."

Lily Vonn doesn't exactly look tough. She's twelve like me, but she looks younger. She's short and thin and kind of cute. She has chin-length blond hair with bangs that go straight across her forehead.

The strange thing about Lily is her eyes. One is blue and one is green. No one can really believe she has two different colors — until they see them.

I brushed most of the snow off the front of my coat and the knees of my jeans. Lily handed me my guitar case. "Hope it's waterproof," she muttered.

I raised my eyes to the street. The dogs were barking wildly again, chasing a squirrel through several front yards.

"I saw you from my window," Lily said as we started toward her house. "Why do they always chase after you?"

I shrugged. "I was just asking myself the same question," I told her. Our boots made crunching noises in the snow. Lily led the way. I stepped in her bootprints.

We waited for a car to move past, its tires sliding on the slick road. Then we crossed the street and made our way up her driveway.

"How come you're late?" Lily asked.

"I had to help my dad shovel the drive," I replied. Some snow had caught inside my hood and was trickling down the back of my neck. I shivered. I couldn't wait to get inside the house.

The others were all hanging out in Lily's living room. I waved hi to Manny, Jared, and Kristina. Manny was down on his knees, fiddling with his guitar amp. It made a loud squeal, and everybody jumped.

Manny is tall and skinny and kind of goofy-looking, with a crooked smile and a mop of curly, black hair. Jared is twelve like the rest of us, but he looks eight. I don't think I've ever seen him without his black-and-silver Raiders cap on. Kristina is a little chubby. She has curly, carrot-colored hair and wears glasses with blue plastic frames.

I tugged off my wet coat and hung it on a peg in the front entryway. The house felt steamy and warm. I straightened my sweatshirt and joined the others.

Manny glanced up from his amp and laughed. "Hey, look — Larry's hair is messed up. Somebody take a picture!"

Everybody laughed.

They're always teasing me about my hair. Can I help it if I have really good hair? It's dark blond and wavy, and I wear it long.

"Hairy Larry!" Lily declared.

The other three laughed and then picked up the

chant. "Hairy Larry! Hairy Larry! Hairy Larry!"

I made an angry face and swept my hand back through my hair, pushing it off my forehead. I could feel myself blushing.

I really don't like being teased. It always makes me angry, and I always blush.

I guess that's why Lily and my other friends tease me so much. They tease me about my hair, and about my big ears, and about anything else they can think of.

And I always get angry. And I always blush. Which makes them tease me even more.

"Hairy Larry! Hairy Larry! Hairy Larry!"

Great friends, huh?

Well, actually, they *are* great friends. We have a lot of fun together. The five of us have a band. This week, it's called The Geeks. Last week, we called ourselves The Spirit. We change the name a lot.

Lily has a gold coin that she wears on a chain around her neck. Her grandfather gave the coin to her. He told her it's real pirate gold.

So Lily wants to call our band Pirate Gold. But I don't think that's cool enough. And Manny, Jared, and Kristina agree.

At least our name — The Geeks — is a lot cooler than Howie and the Shouters. That's the band who's challenging us in the big Battle of the Bands contest at school.

We still can't believe that Howie Hurwin named

7

the band after himself! He's only the drummer. His stuck-up sister, Marissa, is the singer. "Why didn't you call it Marissa and the Shouters?" I asked him one day after school.

"Because Marissa doesn't rhyme with anything," he replied.

"Huh? What does Howie rhyme with?" I asked him.

"Zowie!" he said. Then he laughed and messed up my hair.

What a creep.

No one likes Howie or his sister. The Geeks can't wait to blow the Shouters off the stage.

"If only one of us played bass," Jared moaned as we tuned up.

"Or saxophone or trumpet or something," Kristina added, pulling out a couple of pink guitar picks from her open case.

"I think we sound great," Manny said, still down on the floor, fiddling with the cord to his amp. "Three guitars is a great sound. Especially when we put on the fuzztone and crank them all the way up."

Kristina, Manny, and I all play guitar. Lily is the singer. And Jared plays a keyboard. His keyboard has a drum synthesizer with ten different rhythms on it. So we also have drums. Kind of.

As soon as Manny got his amp working, we tried to play a Rolling Stones song. Jared couldn't find the right drum rhythm on his synthesizer. So we played without it.

As soon as we finished, I shouted, "Let's start again!"

The others all groaned. "Larry, we sounded great!" Lily insisted. "We don't need to play it again."

"The rhythm was way off," I said.

"*You're* way off!" Manny exclaimed, making a face at me.

"Larry is a perfectionist," Kristina said. "Did you forget that, Manny?"

"How could I forget?" Manny groaned. "He never lets us finish one song!"

I could feel myself blushing again. "I just want to get it right," I told them.

Okay. Okay. Maybe I *am* a perfectionist. Is that a bad thing?

"The Battle of the Bands is in two weeks," I said. "We don't want to get onstage and embarrass ourselves, do we?"

I just *hate* being embarrassed. I hate it more than anything in the world. More than steamed broccoli!

We started playing again. Jared hit the saxophone button on his keyboard, and it sounded as if we had a saxophone. Manny took the first solo, and I took the second.

I messed up one chord. I wanted to start again.

But I knew they'd *murder* me if I stopped. So I kept on playing.

Lily's voice cracked on a high note. But she has such a sweet, tiny voice, it didn't sound too bad.

We played without taking a break for nearly two hours. It sounded pretty good. Whenever Jared found the right drum rhythm, it sounded *really* good.

After we put our instruments back in their cases, Lily suggested we go outside and mess around in the snow. The afternoon sun was still high in a shimmery blue sky. The thick blanket of snow sparkled in the golden sunlight.

We chased each other around the snow-covered evergreen shrubs in Lily's front yard. Manny crushed a big, wet snowball over Jared's Raiders cap. That started a snowball fight that lasted until we were all gasping for breath and laughing too hard to toss any more snow.

"Let's build a snowman," Lily suggested.

"Let's make it look like Larry," Kristina added. Her blue-framed glasses were completely steamed up.

"Whoever heard of a snowman with perfect blond hair?" Lily replied.

"Give me a break," I muttered.

They started to roll big balls of snow for the snowman's body. Jared shoved Manny over one of the big snowballs and tried to roll him up in the ball. But Manny was too heavy. The whole thing crumbled to powder under him.

While they worked on the snowman, I wandered down to the street. Something caught my eye at the curb next door.

A pile of junk standing next to a metal trash Dumpster.

I glanced up at the neighbors' house. I could see that it was being remodeled. The pile of junk at the curb was waiting to be carted away.

I leaned over the side of the Dumpster and began shuffling through the stuff. I love old junk. I can't help myself. I just love pawing through piles of old stuff.

Leaning into the Dumpster, I shoved aside a stack of wall tiles and a balled-up shower curtain. Beneath a small, round, shag rug, I found a white enamel medicine chest.

"Wow! This is cool!" I murmured to myself.

I pulled it up with both hands, moved away from the Dumpster, and opened the chest. To my surprise, I found bottles and plastic tubes inside.

I started to examine them, moving them around with my hand, when an orange bottle caught my eye. "Hey, guys!" I shouted up to my friends. "Look what I found!"

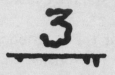

I carried the orange bottle back up to Lily's yard. "Hey, guys — look!" I called, waving the bottle.

No one looked up. Manny and Jared were struggling to lift one big snowball and set it on the other one to form the snowman's body. Lily was shouting encouragement. Kristina was wiping snow off her glasses with one of her gloves.

"Hey, Larry — what's that?" Kristina finally asked, putting her glasses back on. The others turned and saw the bottle in my hand.

I read the label to them: "INSTA-TAN. Rub on a dark suntan in minutes."

"Cool!" Manny declared. "Let's try it."

"Where did you find it?" Lily demanded. Her cheeks were bright red from the cold. There were white flecks of snow in her bangs.

I pointed to the Dumpster. "Your neighbors threw it out. The bottle is full," I announced.

"Let's try it!" Manny repeated, grinning his crooked grin.

"Yeah. Let's all go into school on Monday with dark suntans!" Kristina urged. "Can you see the look on Miss Shindling's face? We'll tell her we all went to Florida!"

"No! The Bahamas!' Lily declared. "We'll tell Howie Hurwin that The Geeks went to the Bahamas to practice!"

Everyone laughed.

"Do you think the stuff works?" Jared asked, adjusting his cap and staring at the bottle.

"It *has* to," Lily said. "They couldn't sell it if it didn't work." She grabbed the bottle from my hand. "It's nearly full. We can all get great tans. Come on. Let's do it. It'll be so cool!"

We all followed Lily back into the house, our boots crunching over the snow, our breath steaming up above our heads.

I pulled off my coat and tossed it onto the pile with the others. As I made my way into the living room, I began to have second thoughts. What if the stuff doesn't work? I asked myself. What if it turns us bright yellow or green instead of tan?

I'd be so totally embarrassed if I had to show up at school with bright green skin. I couldn't do it. I just couldn't. Even if it took months, I'd hide in my house — in my closet — till the stuff wore off.

The others didn't seem to be worried.

We jammed into the downstairs bathroom. Lily still had the bottle of INSTA-TAN. She twisted off the cap and poured a big glob of it into her hand. It was a creamy white liquid.

"Mmmmm. Smells nice," Lily reported, raising her hand to her face. "Very sweet-smelling."

She began rubbing it on her neck, then her cheeks, then her forehead. Tilting the bottle, she poured another big puddle into her palm. Then she rubbed the liquid over the backs of both hands.

Manny took the INSTA-TAN bottle next. He splashed a big glob of it into his hand. Then he started rubbing it all over his face.

"Feels cool and creamy," Kristina reported when her turn came. Jared went next. He practically emptied the bottle as he rubbed the stuff on his face and neck.

Finally it was my turn. I took the bottle and started to tilt it into my palm.

But something made me stop. I hesitated. I could see that the others were all watching me, waiting for me to splash the liquid all over my skin, too.

But, instead, I turned the bottle over and read the tiny print on the label.

And what I read made me gasp out loud.

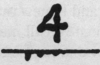

# 4

"Larry, what's your problem?" Lily demanded. "Just pour a little in your hand and rub it on."

"But — but — but — " I sputtered.

"Do I look darker?" Kristina asked Lily. "Is it working?"

"Not yet," Lily told her. She turned back to me. "What's wrong, Larry?"

"The l-label," I stammered. "It says 'Do not use after February, 1991.' "

Everyone laughed. Their laughter rang off the tile walls in the narrow bathroom.

"It can't hurt you," Lily said, shaking her head. "So *what* if the stuff is a little old? That doesn't mean it will make your skin fall off!"

"Don't wimp out," Manny said, grabbing the bottle and tilting the top toward my hand. "Go ahead. Pour it. We've all done it, Larry. Now it's your turn."

"I think my skin is starting to tan," Kristina

said. She and Jared were admiring themselves in the mirror over the sink.

"Go ahead, Larry," Lily urged. "Those dates on the labels don't mean anything." She shoved my arm. "Put it on. What could happen?"

I could see that they were all staring at me now. My face grew hot, and I knew that I was blushing.

I didn't want them to call me a wimp. I didn't want to be the only one to chicken out. So I tilted the bottle down and poured the last sticky glob of the liquid into the palm of my hand.

Then I splashed it onto my face and rubbed it all over. I covered my face, my neck, and the back of my hands. It felt cool and creamy. And it did have a sweet smell, a little like my dad's aftershave.

The others cheered when I finished rubbing the cream in. "Way to go, Larry!" Jared clapped me on the back so hard, I nearly dropped the empty INSTA-TAN bottle.

We all pushed and shoved, struggling to get a good view of ourselves in the small medicine chest mirror. Manny gave Jared a hard shove and sent him sprawling into the shower.

"How long is it supposed to take?" Kristina asked. The bright ceiling light reflected off her glasses as she studied herself in the mirror.

"I don't think it's working at all," Lily said, letting out a disappointed sigh.

I studied the label again. "It says we should

16

have a dark, good-looking tan almost instantly," I reported. I shook my head. "I knew this stuff was too old. I knew we shouldn't have — "

Manny's shrill scream cut off my words. We all turned to him and saw his horrified expression.

"My face!" Manny shrieked. "My face! It's falling off!"

He had his hands cupped. They trembled as he held them up. And I saw that he was holding a pale blob of his own skin!

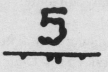

## 5

"Ohhhh." A weak moan escaped my lips.

The others stared down at Manny's hands in silent horror.

"My skin!" he groaned. "My skin!"

And then a grin burst out over his face, and he started to laugh.

As he held up his hand, I saw that it wasn't a piece of pale skin at all. It was a wet, wadded-up tissue.

Laughing his head off, Manny let the tissue float down to the bathroom floor.

"You jerk!" Lily cried angrily.

We all began shouting and shoving Manny. We pushed him into the shower. Lily reached for the knobs to turn on the water.

"No — stop!" Manny pleaded, laughing hard, struggling to break free. "Please! It was just a joke!"

Lily changed her mind and backed away. We

all took final glances into the mirror as we paraded out of the bathroom.

No change. No tan. The stuff hadn't worked at all.

We grabbed our coats and hurried back outside to finish the snowman. I took the empty INSTA-TAN bottle with me and tossed it into the snow as Lily and Kristina rolled a snowball to make the head. Then they lifted it onto the snowman's body.

I found two dark stones for eyes. Manny grabbed Jared's Raiders cap and placed it on the snowman's head. It looked pretty good, but Jared quickly grabbed his cap back.

"It looks a lot like you, Manny," Jared said. "Except smarter."

We all laughed.

A strong gust of wind whipped around the side of the house. The wind toppled the snowman's head. It rolled off the body and crumbled to powder on the ground.

"Now it *really* looks like you!" Jared told Manny.

"Think fast!" Manny cried. He scooped up a big handful of snow and heaved it at Jared.

Jared tried to duck. But the snow poured over him. He instantly bent down, scooped up an even bigger pile of snow, and dropped it over Manny's head.

This started a long, funny, snowball fight among

the five of us. Actually, it turned out to be Lily and me against Manny, Jared, and Kristina.

The two of us held our own for a while. Lily is the fastest snowball maker I ever saw. She can make one and throw it in the time it takes me to bend down and start rolling the snow between my gloves.

The snowball fight quickly became a war. We weren't even bothering to make snowballs. We were just heaving big handfuls of snow at each other. And then we started rolling in the snow. And then we chased each other to the next yard, where the snow was fresh — and started another heavy-duty snowball fight.

What a great time! We were laughing and shouting, all breathing hard, all steaming hot despite the cold, swirling winds.

And then suddenly I felt sick.

I dropped to my knees, swallowing hard. The snow started to gleam brightly. Too brightly. The ground swayed and shook.

I felt *really* sick.

What's happening to me? I wondered.

# 6

Dr. Murkin raised the long hypodermic needle. It gleamed in the light. A tiny droplet of green liquid spilled from the tip.

"Take a deep breath and hold it, Larry," the doctor instructed in his whispery voice. "This won't hurt."

He said the same words every time I had to see him.

I knew he was lying. The shot hurt. It hurt every time I got one, which was about every two weeks.

He grabbed my arm gently with his free hand. He leaned close to me, so close I could smell the peppermint mouthwash on his breath.

I took a deep breath and turned away. I could never bear to watch the long needle sink into my arm.

"Ow!" I let out a low cry as the needle punctured the skin.

Dr. Murkin tightened his grip on my arm. "That

21

doesn't hurt much, does it?" he asked, his voice just above a whisper.

"Not too much," I groaned.

I glanced up at my mother. She was biting her lower lip, her face twisted in worry. She looked as if *she* were getting the shot!

Finally, I felt the needle slide out. Dr. Murkin dabbed a cold, alcohol-soaked cotton ball against the puncture spot. "You'll be okay now," he said, patting my bare back. "You can put your shirt back on."

He turned and smiled reassuringly at my mother.

Dr. Murkin is a very distinguished-looking man. I guess he's about fifty or so. He has straight white hair that he slicks down and brushes straight back. He has friendly blue eyes behind square-shaped, black eyeglasses, and a warm smile.

Even though he lies when he says the shot won't hurt, I think he's a really good doctor, and I like him a lot. He always makes me feel better.

"Same old sweat gland problem," he told my mother, writing some notes in my file. "He got overheated. And we know that's not good — don't we, Larry?"

I muttered a reply.

I have a problem with my sweat glands. They don't work very well. I mean, I can't sweat. So when I get really overheated, I start to feel sick.

That's why I have to see Dr. Murkin every two

weeks. He gives me shots that make me feel better.

Our snowball battle was a lot of fun. But out in the snow and cold wind, I didn't even realize I was getting overheated.

That's why I started to feel weird.

"Do you feel better now?" my mom asked as we made our way out of the doctor's office.

I nodded. "Yeah. I'm okay," I told her. I stopped at the door and turned to face her. "Do I look any different, Mom?"

"Huh?" She narrowed her dark eyes at me. "Different? How?"

"Do I look like maybe I have a suntan or something?" I asked hopefully.

Her eyes studied my face. "I'm a little worried about you, Larry," she said quietly. "I want you to take a short nap when we get home. Okay?"

I guessed that meant I didn't look too tanned.

I *knew* that INSTA-TAN wouldn't work. The bottle was too old. And it probably didn't work even when it was new.

"It's hard to get a suntan in the winter," Mom commented as we headed across the snowy parking lot to the car.

Tell me about it, I thought, rolling my eyes.

Lily called me right after dinner. "I felt a little sick, too," she admitted. "Are you okay?"

"Yeah. I'm fine," I replied. I held the cordless

phone in one hand and flipped TV channels with the remote control in my other hand.

It's a bad habit of mine. Sometimes I flip channels for hours at a time and never really watch anything.

"Howie and Marissa walked by after you left," Lily said.

"Did you massacre them?" I asked eagerly. "Did you bury them in snowballs?"

Lily laughed. "No. We were all soaked and exhausted by the time Howie and Marissa showed up. We all just sort of stood there, shivering."

"Did Howie say anything about their band?" I asked.

"Yeah," Lily replied. "He said he bought an Eric Clapton guitar book. He said he's learning some new songs that will blow us away."

"Howie should stick to drums. He is the worst guitar player in the world," I muttered. "When he plays, the guitar actually *squeaks*! I don't know how he does it. How do you make a guitar squeak?"

Lily laughed. "Marissa squeaks, too. But she calls it singing!"

We both laughed.

I cut my laughter short. "Do you think Howie and the Shouters are any good?"

"I don't know," Lily replied thoughtfully. "Howie brags so much, you can't really believe him. He says they're good enough to make a CD.

24

He says his dad wants them to make a demo tape so he can send it to all the big CD companies."

"Yeah. Sure," I muttered sarcastically. "We should sneak over to Howie's house some afternoon when they're all practicing," I suggested. "We could listen at the window. Check them out."

"Marissa is actually a pretty good singer," Lily said. "She has a nice voice."

"But she's not as good as you," I said.

"Well, I think we're getting better," Lily commented. Then she added, "It's a shame we don't have a real drummer."

I agreed. "Jared's drum machine doesn't always play the same song we play!"

Lily and I talked about the Battle of the Bands a while longer. Then I said good night, turned off the phone, and sat down at my desk to start my homework.

I didn't finish until nearly ten. Yawning, I went downstairs to tell Mom and Dad I was going to sleep. Back upstairs, I changed into pajamas and crossed the hall to the bathroom to brush my teeth.

Under the bright bathroom light, I studied my face in the mirror over the sink. No tan. My face stared back at me, as pale as ever.

I picked up my toothbrush and spread a small line of blue toothpaste on it.

I started to raise the toothbrush to my mouth — and then stopped.

"Hey — !" I cried out.

The toothbrush dropped into the sink as I gazed at the back of my hand.

At first I thought the hand was covered by a dark shadow.

But as I raised it closer to my face, I saw to my horror that it was no shadow.

I let out a loud gulping sound as I stared at the back of my hand.

It was covered by a patch of thick, black hair.

# 7

Staring down in shock, I shook the hand hard. I think I expected the black hair to fall off.

I grabbed at it with my other hand and tugged it.

"Ow!"

The hair really was growing from the back of my hand.

"How can this be?" I cried to myself. Holding the hand in the light, I struggled to stop it from trembling so that I could examine it.

The hair was nearly half an inch high. It was shiny and black. Very spikey. Very prickly. It felt kind of rough as I rubbed my other hand over it.

"Hairy Larry."

That dumb name Lily called me suddenly popped back into my head.

"Hairy Larry."

In the mirror I could see my face turning red. They'll call me Hairy Larry for the rest of my life,

27

I thought unhappily, if they ever see this black hair growing out of my hand!

I *can't* let anyone see this! I told myself, feeling my chest tighten in panic. I *can't*! It would be so embarrassing!

I examined my left hand. It was as smooth and clear as ever.

"Thank goodness it's only on one hand!" I cried.

I tugged frantically at the patch of black hair again. I pulled at it until my hand ached. But the hair didn't come out.

My mouth suddenly felt dry. I gripped the edge of the sink with both hands, struggling to stop my entire body from trembling.

"What am I going to do?" I murmured.

Do I have to wear a glove for the rest of my life?

I can't let my friends see this. They'll call me Hairy Larry forever. That's how I'll be known for the rest of my life!

A panicky sob escaped my throat.

Got to calm down, I warned myself. Got to think clearly.

I was gripping the sink so tightly, my hands ached. I lifted them, then rolled up both pajama sleeves.

Were my arms covered in black hair, too?
No.
I let out a long sigh of relief.
The square patch of prickly hair on the back of

my right hand seemed to be the only hair that had grown.

What to do? What to do?

I could hear my parents climbing the stairs, on their way to their bedroom. Quickly, I closed the bathroom door and locked it.

"Larry — are you still up? I thought you went to bed," I heard my mom call from out in the hall.

"Just brushing my hair!" I called out.

I brush my hair every night before I go to bed.

I know it doesn't make any sense. I know it gets messed up the instant I put my head down on the pillow.

It's just a weird habit.

I raised my eyes to my hair. My dark blond hair, so soft and wavy.

So unlike the disgusting patch of spikey black hair on my hand.

I felt sick. My stomach hurtled up to my throat.

I forced back my feeling of nausea and pulled open the door to the medicine chest. My eyes slid desperately over the bottles and tubes.

Hair Remover. I searched for the words Hair Remover.

There *is* such a thing — isn't there?

Not in our medicine cabinet. I read every jar, every bottle. No Hair Remover.

I stared down at the black patch on my hand. Had the hair grown a little bit? Or was I imagining it?

Another idea flashed into my mind.

I pulled down my dad's razor. On the bottom shelf of the medicine cabinet, I found a can of shaving cream.

I'll shave it all off, I decided. It will be easy.

I'd watched my dad shave a million times. There was nothing to it. I started the hot water running in the sink. I splashed some onto the back of my hand. Then I rubbed the bar of soap over the bristly black hair until it got all lathery.

My hands were wet and slippery, and the can of shaving cream nearly slid out of my grip. But I managed to push the top and spray a pile of white shaving cream onto the back of my hand.

I smoothed it over the ugly black hair. Then I picked up the razor in my left hand, held it under the hot water, the way I'd seen Dad do it.

And I started to shave. It was so hard to shave with my left hand.

The razor blade slid over the thick patch. The bristly hair came right off.

I watched it flow down the sink drain.

Then I held my hand under the faucet and let the water rinse away the rest of the shaving cream lather.

The water felt warm and soothing. I dried off my hand and then examined it carefully.

Smooth. Smooth and clean.

Not a trace of the disgusting black hair.

Feeling a lot better, I put my dad's razor and

shaving cream back in the medicine chest. Then I crept across the hall to my bedroom.

Rubbing the back of my hand, enjoying its cool smoothness, I clicked off the ceiling light and climbed into bed.

My head sank heavily into the pillow. I yawned, suddenly feeling really sleepy.

What had caused that ugly hair to grow? The question had been nagging at me ever since I discovered it.

Was it the INSTA-TAN? Was it that old bottle of tanning lotion?

I wondered if any of my friends had grown hair, too? I had to giggle as I pictured Manny covered in hair, like a big gorilla.

But it wasn't funny. It was scary.

I rubbed my hand. Still smooth. The hair didn't seem to be growing back.

I yawned again, drifting to sleep.

Oh, no. I'm itchy, I suddenly realized, half-awake, half-asleep. My whole body feels itchy.

Is spikey black hair growing all over my body?

"Did you sleep?" Mom asked as I dragged myself into the kitchen for breakfast. "You look pale."

Dad lowered his newspaper to check me out. A white mug of coffee steamed in front of him. "He doesn't look pale to me," he muttered before returning to his newspaper.

"I slept okay," I said, sliding on to the stool at the breakfast counter. I studied my hand, keeping it under the counter just in case.

No hair. It looked perfectly smooth.

I had jumped out of bed the instant Mom called from downstairs. I turned on the light and studied my entire body in front of my dresser mirror.

No black hair.

I was so happy, I felt like singing. I felt like hugging Mom and Dad and doing a dance on the breakfast table.

But that would be embarrassing.

So I happily ate my Frosted Flakes and drank my orange juice.

Mom sat down beside Dad and started to crack open a hard-boiled egg. She had a hard-boiled egg every morning. But she threw away the yellow and only ate the white. She said she didn't want the cholesterol.

"Mom and Dad, I have to tell you something. I did a pretty stupid thing yesterday. I found an old bottle of a cream called INSTA-TAN in a trash Dumpster. And my friends and I all rubbed it on ourselves. You know. So we'd have tans. But the date had run out on the bottle. And . . . well . . . last night, I suddenly grew some really gross black hair on the back of my hand."

That's what I *wanted* to say.

I wanted to tell them about it. I even opened my mouth to start telling them. But I couldn't do it.

I'd be so embarrassed.

They would just start yelling at me and telling me what a jerk I was. They'd probably drag me off to Dr. Murkin and tell him what I had done. And then *he* would tell me how stupid I had been.

So I kept my mouth shut.

"You're awfully quiet this morning," Mom said, sliding a sliver of egg white into her mouth.

"Nothing much to talk about," I muttered.

I ran into Lily on the way to school. She had her coat collar pulled up and a red-and-blue wool ski cap pulled down over her short blond hair.

"It isn't *that* cold!" I said, jogging to catch up with her.

"Mom said it's going down to ten," Lily replied. "She made me bundle up."

The morning sun floated low over the houses, a red ball in the pale sky. The wind felt sharp. We leaned into it as we walked. A hard crust had formed over the snow, and our boots crunched loudly.

I took a deep breath. I decided to ask Lily the big question on my mind. "Lily," I started hesitantly. "Did any . . . uh . . . well . . . did any strange hair grow on the back of your hands last night?"

She stopped walking and stared at me. A solemn expression darkened her face. "Yes," she confessed in a hushed whisper.

# 9

"Huh?" I gasped. My heart skipped a beat. "You grew hair on your hand?"

Lily nodded grimly. She moved closer. Her blue eye and her green eye stared at me from under the wool ski cap.

"Hair grew on my hands," she whispered, her breath steaming up the cold air as she talked. "Then it grew on my arms, and my legs, and my back."

I let out a choked cry.

"Then my face changed into a wolf's face," Lily continued, still staring hard at me. "And I ran out to the woods and howled at the moon. Like this." She threw back her head and uttered a long, mournful howl.

"Then I found three people in the woods, and I *ate* them!" Lily declared. "Because I'm a *werewolf!*"

She growled at me and snapped her teeth. And then she burst out laughing.

I could feel my face turning red.

Lily gave me a hard, playful shove. I lost my balance and nearly fell on to my back.

She laughed even harder. "You *believed* me — didn't you, Larry!" she accused. "You actually believed that dumb story!"

"No way!" I cried. My face felt red-hot. "No way, Lily. Of *course* I didn't believe you!"

But I *had* believed her story. Up to the part where she said she ate three people.

Then I finally figured out that she was joking, that she was teasing me.

"Hairy Larry!" Lily chanted. "Hairy Larry!"

"Stop it!" I insisted angrily. "You're not funny, you know? You're not funny at all!"

"Well, *you* are!" she shot back. "Funny-looking!"

"Ha-ha," I replied sarcastically. I turned and crossed the street, taking long strides, trying to get away from her.

"Hairy Larry!" she called, chasing after me. "Hairy Larry!"

I slid on a patch of ice. I quickly caught my balance, but my backpack slid off my shoulder and dropped with a *thud* onto the street.

As I bent to pick it up, Lily stood over me. "Did *you* grow hair last night, Larry?" she demanded.

"Huh?" I pretended not to hear her.

"Did you grow hair on the back of your hand?

Is that why you asked me?" Lily asked, leaning over me.

"No way," I muttered. I hoisted the backpack onto my shoulder and started walking again. "No way," I repeated.

Lily laughed. "Are *you* a werewolf?"

I pretended to laugh, too. "No. I'm a vampire," I replied.

I wished I could tell Lily the truth. I really wanted to tell her about the patch of ugly hair.

But I knew she could never keep it a secret. I knew she would spread the story over the whole school. And then everyone I knew would call me Hairy Larry for the rest of my life!

I felt bad about lying to her. I mean, she *is* my best friend.

But what could I do?

We walked the rest of the way to school without saying much. I kept glancing over at Lily. She had the strangest smile on her face.


"Are you ready to present your book reports?" Miss Shindling asked.

The classroom erupted with sounds — chairs scraping, Trapper-Keepers being opened, papers being rustled, throats being cleared.

Standing in front of the entire class and reciting a book report makes everyone nervous. It makes me *very* nervous! I just hate having everyone stare at me.

And if I goof up a word or forget what I want to say next, I always turn bright red. And then everyone laughs and makes fun of me.

The night before, I had practiced my book report standing in front of the mirror. And I had done pretty well. Only a few tiny mistakes.

Of course, I hadn't been nervous giving the report to myself in my room. Now, my knees were shaking — and I hadn't even been called on yet!

"Howie, would you give your report first?" Miss Shindling asked, motioning for Howie Hurwin to come to the front of the class.

"It's a shame to have the *best* go first!" Howie replied, grinning.

A few kids laughed. Other kids groaned.

I knew that Howie wasn't joking. He really thought he was the best at everything.

He stepped confidently to the front of the room. Howie is a big guy, sort of chubby, with thick, brown hair that he never brushes, and a big, round face with freckles on his cheeks.

He always has a smirk on his face. A stuck-up look that says, "I'm the best — and you're an insect."

He usually wears baggy faded denim jeans about five sizes too big, and a long-sleeved T-shirt with a shiny black vest opened over it.

He held up the book he was reporting on. One of the Matt Christopher baseball books.

I groaned to myself. I knew in advance exactly

what Howie was going to say: "I recommend this book to anyone who likes baseball."

That's how Howie always started his book reports. So boring!

But Howie always got A's anyway. I never understood why Miss Shindling thinks he's so terrific.

Howie cleared his throat and grinned at Miss Shindling. Then he turned to the class and started his report in a loud, steady voice. "I recommend this book to anyone who likes baseball," he began.

Told you.

I yawned loudly. No one seemed to notice.

Howie droned on. "This is a very exciting book with a very good plot," he said. "If you like a lot of excitement, you'll like this book. Especially if you're a baseball fan."

I didn't hear the rest of it. I kept silently going over and over my own book report.

A few minutes later, when Miss Shindling announced, "Larry, you're next!" I almost didn't hear her.

I took a deep breath and climbed to my feet. *Stay cool, Larry*, I told myself. *You've practiced and practiced your report. There's nothing to be nervous about.*

Clearing my throat loudly, I started up the aisle to the front of the room. I was halfway up the aisle when Howie stuck out his foot.

I saw his big grin — but I didn't see his foot.

"Oh!" I cried out in surprise as I stumbled over it — and went sprawling on the floor.

The classroom exploded with laughter.

My heart pounding, I started to pull myself up. But I stopped when I saw my hands.

Both of them were bristling with thick, black hair.

# 10

"Larry, are you okay?" I heard Miss Shindling call from her desk.

"Uh . . ." I was too stunned to answer.

"Larry, are you hurt?"

"Uh . . . well . . ." I couldn't speak at all. I couldn't move. I couldn't think.

Crouched on the floor, I stared in horror at my hairy hands.

Above me, I could hear kids still laughing about how Howie had tripped me. I glanced up to see the kid next to Howie slapping him a high-five.

Ha-ha. Very funny.

Usually, I'd be totally embarrassed. But I didn't have time to be embarrassed. I was too scared.

Had anyone seen my hairy hands?

Still down on the floor, I glanced quickly around the room.

No one was pointing in horror or crying out.

Maybe no one had caught a glimpse of them yet.

Quickly, I jammed both hands deep into my jeans pockets.

When I was sure that both hands were completely hidden, I climbed slowly to my feet.

"Look! Larry is blushing!" someone called from the back row. The room exploded with more laughter.

Of course, that made me blush even redder. But blushing wasn't exactly my biggest problem.

There was *no way* I could stand in front of the class with these two hairy hands. I'd rather die!

Without even thinking about it, I started hurrying back up the aisle to the classroom door. With my hands jammed into my jeans, it wasn't easy to walk fast.

"Larry — what's wrong?" Miss Shindling called from the front of the room. "Where are you going?"

"Uh . . . I'll be right back," I managed to choke out.

"Are you sure you're okay?" the teacher asked.

"Yeah. Fine," I mumbled. "Be right back. Really."

I knew everyone was staring at me. But I didn't care. I just had to get out of there. I had to figure out what to do about my hands.

As I reached the door, I heard Miss Shindling scold Howie. "You could have hurt Larry. You shouldn't trip people, Howie. I've warned you before."

"But, Miss Shindling — it was an accident," Howie lied.

I slipped out the door. Into the long, empty hall.

I checked to make sure no one was around to see me. Then I pulled my hands from my pockets.

I had a dim hope that maybe my hands would be back to normal. But that hope vanished as soon as I raised them to the light.

Thick, black hair — nearly an inch high! — covered both hands. How could it grow so *fast?* I wondered.

The backs of my hands were hairy. And my palms were hairy, too. Hair poked up from the knuckles of my fingers. And clumps of black hair grew in the space *between* my fingers.

I rubbed my hands together, as if trying to rub the ugly hair away. But of course it didn't come off.

"Nooooooo. Please — noooooo!" I moaned out loud without realizing it.

What could I do?

I couldn't go back to class with these hairy monster hands. They would make everyone *sick!*

I would be embarrassed for the rest of my life. Whenever anyone would see me coming, they'd say, "Here comes Hairy Larry Boyd. Remember that day the black hair grew all over his hands?"

I'll run home, I decided. I'll get away from here.

No. How could I leave school in the middle of

the morning? Miss Shindling was waiting for me to return and give my book report.

I stood frozen, my back against the tile wall, gazing at the hideous hands.

And I suddenly realized that I wasn't alone in the hallway.

I glanced up — and gasped when I saw Mr. Fosburg, the principal.

He was carrying a stack of textbooks. But he had stopped a few feet away from me.

And he was staring in shock at my hairy hands.

# 11

I swung my hands down and tucked them behind my back.

But it was too late. Mr. Fosburg had already seen them. His blue eyes narrowed as he studied me.

I shuddered.

What was he going to say? What was he going to do now?

"Is it too cold in the building?" the principal asked.

"Huh?" I replied. What was he asking?

I leaned back against my hands, pressing them against the wall. Even through my shirt, I could feel the prickly hair all over them.

"Should I have the furnace turned up, Larry?" Mr. Fosburg asked. "Is it too cold? Is that why you're wearing gloves to class?"

"G-gloves?" I stammered.

He thought I was wearing gloves!

"Yes. I . . . uh . . . was a little cold," I told

him, starting to feel a little better. "That's why I went to my locker. For gloves."

He stared at me thoughtfully. Then he turned and headed the other way, balancing the stack of textbooks in both hands. "I'll talk to the custodian about it," he called back.

I breathed a sigh of relief as he disappeared around the corner. That had been a close call.

But he had given me a good idea. Gloves.

I hurried to my locker. Turning the dial on the combination lock felt strange with my hairy fingers. But I opened the locker easily and pulled my black leather gloves from the pockets of my parka.

A few seconds later, I stepped back into the classroom. Lily stood at the front of the class, giving her book report. She glanced at me curiously as I slid back into my seat.

When Lily finished, Miss Shindling called me to the front of the room. "Are you okay now, Larry?" she asked.

"Yes," I replied. "My . . . uh . . . hands were cold." I climbed out of my seat and stepped quickly to the front of the room.

Some kids started to giggle and point at my gloves. But I didn't care.

At least no one could see my hands with the ugly black fur sprouting all over them.

I took a deep breath and started my report. "The book I read is by Bruce Coville," I began.

"And I would recommend it to anyone who likes funny science fiction stories. . . ."

After school, I hurried to my locker. I kept my head down and tried to avoid everyone.

I had worn the gloves all day. They were hot and uncomfortable. And they seemed to grow tighter and tighter.

I wondered if the black hair on my hands was growing. But I was afraid to take off the gloves to check it out.

I tugged on my parka and slung my backpack over one shoulder. I have to get out of here and think, I told myself.

A few steps from the front exit, I heard Lily calling my name. I turned and saw her chasing after me. She was wearing an oversized yellow sweater pulled down over bright green tights.

I kept walking. "Catch you later!" I called back to her. "I'm in a hurry."

But she came running up and stepped in front of me. "Aren't you coming to band practice?" she asked.

I was so upset about my hairy hands that I'd completely forgotten.

"It's at my house again this afternoon — remember?" Lily continued, walking backwards as I made my way to the doors.

"I — I can't," I stammered. "I don't feel very well."

That was the truth.

She stared hard at me. "What's your problem, Larry? How come you've been so weird all day?"

"I just don't feel well," I insisted. "Sorry about the practice. Can we do it tomorrow?"

"I guess," she replied. She said something else, but I didn't hear it. I pushed open the door and hurried out of the school.

I ran all the way home. The sun beamed down on the snow, making it gleam like silver. It was beautiful, but I couldn't enjoy it. I was lost in my own troubled thoughts.

Thinking about hair. Thick patches of black, spikey hair.

I burst into the house and tossed my backpack onto the floor. I started up the stairs to my room — but stopped when I heard Mom call my name.

I found her in the living room, on the chair by the front window. She had Jasper, our cat, in her lap and the cordless phone up to her ear. She said something into it, then lowered it as she raised her eyes to me.

"Larry, you're home early. Don't you have band practice?"

"Not today," I lied. "I have a lot of homework, so I came straight home." Another lie.

I didn't want to tell her the truth. I didn't want to tell her that I had rubbed INSTA-TAN all over myself and now I was sprouting disgusting black hair.

I didn't want to tell her. But it suddenly burst out of me. The whole story. I just couldn't hold it in any longer.

"Mom, you won't believe this," I started in a tiny, choked voice. "I'm growing hair, Mom. Really gross black hair. On my hands. You see, my friends and I — we found this old bottle of tanning lotion. And I know it was really stupid. But we all poured it on ourselves. I rubbed it all over my face, and hands, and neck. And now I'm growing hair, Mom. In school today, I looked down. And both of my hands were covered in black hair. I'm so embarrassed. And I'm scared, too. I'm really scared."

I was breathing hard as I finished the story. I had been staring down at the floor as I told it. But now I raised my eyes to see my mom's reaction.

What would she say? Could she help me?

# 12

I heard her mumble something. But I couldn't understand the words.

Then I realized that she wasn't talking to me.

She had the phone pressed to her ear, and she was talking into it.

Mom had gone back to her telephone conversation. She was concentrating so hard, she hadn't heard a word I had said!

I let out an annoyed groan. Then I spun around and hurried up the stairs to my room. I closed the door behind me and tore off the hot, uncomfortable gloves.

Jasper had run upstairs and perched on the windowseat. She spent most of the day on the window seat in my room, staring down at the front yard.

As I tossed the gloves onto a chair, she turned to me. Her bright yellow eyes glowed happily.

I crossed the room and picked her up. Then I sat down on the window seat and hugged her.

"Jasper, you're the only real friend I have," I whispered, petting her back.

To my surprise, the cat let out a squawk, arched her back, and jumped to the floor. She ran halfway across the room, then turned back, her yellow eyes glaring at me.

It took me a few seconds to realize the problem. I held up my hands. "It's these hairy paws, isn't it, Jasper?" I said sadly. "They frightened you — didn't they?"

The cat tilted her head, as if trying to understand me.

"Well, they frighten me, too," I told her.

I jumped up and hurried across the hall to the bathroom. Once again, I pulled my dad's shaving equipment from the medicine cabinet.

I set to work, shaving off the thick hair.

It wasn't easy. Especially trying to shave off the tufts of hair that had grown in the spaces between my fingers. That hair was really hard to reach.

The hair was stiff and tough. Like the bristles on a hairbrush. I cut myself twice, on the palm and the back of my right hand.

As I rinsed the shaving cream off, I glanced down and saw Jasper staring up at me from the bathroom doorway. "Don't tell Mom and Dad," I whispered.

She blinked her yellow eyes and yawned.

The next morning, I awoke before Mom and Dad. Most mornings, I lie in bed and wait for Mom to shout that it's time to get up.

But this morning I jumped out of bed, turned on all the lights, and stepped up to my dresser mirror.

Would I find new hair?

I held up my hands and checked them out first. My eyes were still heavy from sleep. But I could see clearly that the hair had not grown back.

"Yes!" I cried happily.

The razor cuts on my right hand still hurt. But I didn't care. Both hands were smooth and hairless.

I turned them over and gazed at them for a long while. I was so glad they looked normal.

I had dreamed about hair during the night. It had started out as spaghetti. In the dream, I was sitting in the kitchen, starting to eat a big plate of spaghetti.

But as I started to twirl the noodles on my fork, they instantly turned to hair. Long, black hairs.

I was twirling long, black hairs onto my fork. The plate was piled high with long strands of black hair.

Then I raised the forkful of hair to my mouth. I opened my mouth. I brought the hairy fork up closer, closer.

And then I woke up.

Yuck! What a gross dream.

I had felt really sick to my stomach. And it had been hard getting back to sleep.

Now at last it was morning, and I continued my inspection. I leaned over and checked my feet. Then my legs. No black clumps of hair.

No weird fur growing anywhere.

I guess it's safe to go to school, I told myself happily. But I'll be sure to keep my gloves handy.

After breakfast, I pulled on my coat, grabbed my backpack, and headed out of the house.

It was a bright, warm day. The snow glistened wetly. The sunshine had started to melt it. I stepped carefully around puddles of slush as I walked along the sidewalk.

I was feeling better. A lot better. In fact, I was feeling really good.

Then I turned and saw that pack of dogs. Snarling dogs. Heading right for me.

# 13

My heart jumped up to my throat. The dogs were running full speed, their heads bobbing up and down, their eyes trained on me. They barked and growled furiously with each bounding step.

My legs suddenly felt as if they weighed a thousand pounds. But I whirled around and forced myself to run.

If they catch me, they'll tear me to pieces! I told myself. They must smell Jasper on me, I decided. That's why they always chase me.

I loved my cat. But why did she have to get me in so much trouble?

Who owned these vicious dogs, anyway? Why were they allowed to run wild like this?

Questions, questions. They flew through my mind as I ran. Across front yards. Then across the street.

A car horn blared. I heard the squeal of brakes.

A car skidded toward the opposite curb.

I had forgotten to check the traffic before I crossed.

"Sorry!" I called. And kept running.

A sharp pain in my side forced me to slow down. I turned and saw the yapping dogs racing steadily toward me. They crossed the street and kept moving over the snowy ground. Closer. Closer.

"Hey, Larry!" Two kids stepped on to the sidewalk ahead of me.

"Run!" I screamed breathlessly. "The dogs — "

But Lily and Jared didn't move.

I stepped up to them, holding my side. It ached so hard, I could barely breathe.

Lily turned to stare down the dogs, as she had done before. Jared stepped up to meet them. All three of us watched the dogs approach.

Seeing the three of us standing together, the dogs slowed to a stop. The snarls and growls stopped instantly. They stared back at us uncertainly. They were panting hard, their tongues drooping down nearly to the snow.

"Go home!" Lily shouted. She stamped her shoe hard on the sidewalk.

The big black dog, the leader, uttered a low whimper and hung his head.

"Go home! Go home!" All three of us chanted.

The pain in my side started to fade. I felt a little better. The dogs weren't going to attack, I could see. They didn't want to tangle with all three of us.

They turned and started to trot away, following the big black dog.

Suddenly Jared started to laugh. "Look at that one!" he cried. He pointed to a long, scrawny dog with black, curly fur.

"What's so funny about that one?" I demanded.

"He looks just like Manny!" Jared declared.

Lily started to laugh. "You're right! He does!"

All three of us laughed. The dog had Manny's curly hair. And he had Manny's dark, soulful eyes.

"Come on. We'll be late," Lily said. She kicked a hard clump of snow off the sidewalk. Jared and I followed her toward school.

"Why were those dogs chasing you?" Jared asked.

"I think because they smelled my cat," I replied.

"Those dogs are mean," Lily said, a few steps ahead of us. "They shouldn't let them run wild like that."

"Tell me about it," I replied, rolling my eyes.

A sharp gust of wind nearly blew us backwards over the slippery sidewalk. Jared's Raiders cap went flying into the street. A station wagon rumbled past, nearly running it over.

Jared darted into the street and snatched the cap back. "I'll be glad when winter is over," he muttered.

We met Kristina in front of the school. Her red hair blew wildly around her head in the swirling wind. "Do we have band practice this afternoon?" she asked. She was chewing a Snickers bar.

"Great breakfast," I said sarcastically.

"Mom didn't have time to make eggs," Kristina replied, chewing.

"Yes. Practice at my house," Lily said. "We've got to get to work, guys. We don't want Howie to win the contest."

Kristina turned to me. "Where were you yesterday?"

"I . . . uh . . . didn't feel too well," I replied.

That reminded me of the INSTA-TAN lotion. Were any of my friends growing hair, too, because of that suntan gunk? I had to know. I had to ask.

But if they weren't growing hair — if I was the only one — then I'd be totally embarrassed.

"Uh . . . remember that INSTA-TAN stuff?" I asked quietly.

"Great stuff," Jared replied. "I think it made me paler!"

Kristina laughed. "It didn't work at all. You were right, Larry. That bottle was too old."

"Look at us," Lily added. "We're all as pale as the snow. That stuff didn't do anything."

*But are you growing weird black patches of hair now?*

That's what I was dying to ask.

But none of them said anything about growing hair.

Were they like me? Were they too embarrassed to admit it?

Or was I the only one?

I took a deep breath. Should I ask? Should I ask if anyone was sprouting hair?

I opened my mouth to ask. But I stopped when I realized that the subject had changed. They were talking about our band again.

"Can you bring your amp to my house?" Lily asked Kristina. "Manny will bring his. But it only has jacks to plug in two guitars."

"Maybe I can bring mine — " I started to say.

But a gust of wind blew my parka hood back.

I reached up to pull the hood back on my head.

But my hand brushed the back of my neck — and I gasped.

The back of my neck was covered with thick hair.

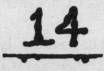

# 14

"Larry — what's wrong?" Lily demanded.

"Uh . . . uh . . ." I couldn't speak.

"What's wrong with your scarf?" Jared asked. "Is it too tight?" He tugged at the wool scarf around my neck.

The scratchy scarf my mom made me wear because my great-aunt Hildy had knitted it.

I had forgotten I was wearing it. When my hand brushed against it, I'd thought . . .

"You looked scared to death!" Lily exclaimed. "Are you okay, Larry?"

I nodded. "Yeah. I'm okay," I muttered, feeling my face go red. "The scarf was choking me, I guess." What a lame lie.

But I had to say *something*. I couldn't say that I had mistakenly thought that my neck had sprouted fur!

Larry, you've got to stop thinking about hair! I scolded myself. If you don't, you'll drive yourself crazy!

I shivered. "Let's go inside," I said, wrapping the wool scarf tightly around my neck.

I hurried to the boys' room to brush my hair before the bell rang. Gazing at my wavy, blond hair in the mirror as I brushed it, I had a horrifying thought.

What if my real hair suddenly fell out? And the gross, prickly black hair grew in its place?

What if I woke up one morning, and my entire head was covered in the disgusting black fur?

I took a long look at myself in the mirror. Someone had smeared soap over the glass, and my reflection appeared to stare back through hazy, white streaks.

"Shape up," I told myself.

I pointed a finger at my reflection. A smooth, hairless finger.

"Stop thinking about hair, Larry," I instructed my reflection. "Stop thinking about it. You're going to be okay."

The INSTA-TAN lotion has worn off, I decided.

It had been several days since my friends and I had splashed it on ourselves. I had taken at least three showers and two baths.

It wore off, I told myself. It's all gone. Stop worrying about it.

I took one last glance at my hair. It was getting pretty long, but I liked it that way. I liked brushing the sides back over my ears.

Maybe I'll let it grow *really* long, I thought. I tucked the hairbrush into my backpack and headed to class.

I had a pretty good day until Miss Shindling handed back the history term papers.

It wasn't the grade that upset me. She gave me a ninety-four, which is really good. I knew that Lily would probably brag that she got a ninety-eight or a ninety-nine. But Lily was great at writing.

A ninety-four was really excellent for me.

The grade made me happy. But when I flipped through the pages, glancing over Miss Shindling's comments on my writing, I found a black hair on page three.

Was it *my* black hair? I wondered. Was it one of the disgusting black hairs that had sprouted on my hands?

Or was it Miss Shindling's? Miss Shindling had short, straight black hair. It *could* be one of hers.

Or else . . .

I squinted at the hair, afraid to touch it.

I knew I was starting to get weird. I knew I had made a solemn vow that I was going to stop thinking about hair.

But I couldn't help it.

Seeing this one, stubby little black hair stuck to the third page of my term paper gave me the shudders. Finally, I raised the term paper close to my face — and blew the hair away.

I didn't hear a word Miss Shindling said for the rest of the class. I was glad when the bell rang and it was time to go to gym.

It will feel good to run around and get some exercise, I decided.

"Basketball today!" Coach Rafferty shouted as we filed into the brightly lit gym. "Basketball today! Change into your shorts! Come on — hustle!"

I usually don't like basketball that much. There's so much running back and forth. Back and forth the entire length of the floor. Also, I don't have a very good shooting eye. And I get really embarrassed when a teammate passes me the ball and I miss an easy shot.

But, today, basketball sounded just right. A chance to run and get rid of a lot of my nervous energy.

I followed the other guys into the locker room. We all opened our gym lockers and pulled out our shorts and T-shirts.

At the end of the row of lockers, Howie Hurwin kept shouting, "In your face! In your face!"

Another guy snapped a towel at Howie.

Serves him right, I thought. Howie is such a jerk.

"In your face!" I heard Howie chant. Someone shouted to him to shut up.

"In your face, man! In your face!"

I sat down on the bench and pulled off my sneakers. Then I stood up and started to pull off my jeans.

I stopped when I got the jeans about halfway down.

I stopped and let out a low cry when I saw my knees.

Bushy clumps of furry black hair had sprouted from both knees.

## 15

"How come you kept your jeans on in gym?" Jared asked.

"Huh?" His question caught me by surprise. It was the next day, and we were walking along the slushy sidewalks, lugging our instruments to Lily's house for another band practice.

"You refused to change into gym shorts, remember?" Jared said, swinging his keyboard case at his side.

"I . . . was just cold," I told him. "My legs got cold. That's all. I don't know why Coach Rafferty gave me such a hard time."

Jared laughed. "Rafferty nearly swallowed his whistle when you sank that three-point jump shot from midcourt!"

I laughed, too. I am the worst shot in school. But I was so crazed about my hairy knees, so totally *pumped*, that I played better than I'd ever played in my life.

"Maybe you should wear jeans *all* the time!" Coach Rafferty had joked.

But, of course, it was no joke.

I ran all the way home after school and spent nearly half an hour locked in the upstairs bathroom, shaving the clumps of black hair off my knees.

When I finally finished, both knees were red and sore. But at least they were smooth again.

I spent the rest of the afternoon closed up in my room, thinking hard about what was happening to me. Unfortunately, all I came up with were questions. Dozens of questions.

But no answers.

Sprawled on my stomach on top of the bed, my knees throbbed as I thought. Why did my knees grow hair? I asked myself. I didn't spread any INSTA-TAN on my knees. So why did the ugly black hair sprout there?

Had the INSTA-TAN worked itself into my system? Had the strange liquid seeped into my pores? Had it spread through my entire body?

Was I going to turn into some kind of big, hairy creature? Was I soon going to look like King Kong or something?

Questions — but no answers.

The questions still troubled me as I crossed the street with Jared, and Lily's white-frame house came into view on the corner.

The sun beamed down above the two bare maple trees that leaned over Lily's driveway. The air felt warm, almost like spring. The snow had melted a lot in one day. Patches of wet grass poked up through the white.

In the yard across the street from Lily's house, a half-melted snowman looked sad and droopy. My hightops splashed through the slushy puddles as Jared and I carried our instruments up the driveway.

Lily opened the door for us. She and Kristina had already been practicing. Lily was wearing a bright red-and-blue ski sweater pulled down over pale blue leggings. Kristina wore faded jeans and a green-and-gold Notre Dame sweatshirt.

"Where's Manny?" Lily asked, closing the front door behind Jared and me.

"Haven't seen him," I replied, scraping my wet sneakers on the floor mat. "Isn't he here?"

"He wasn't in school again today," Kristina reported.

"We've got to get serious," Lily said, biting her lower lip. "Did you talk to Howie today? Did he tell you what his dad bought him?"

"A new synthesizer?" I replied, bending to open my guitar case. "Yeah. Howie told me all about it. He says it can sound like an entire orchestra."

"Who wants to sound like an orchestra?" Jared asked. He had a wet leaf stuck to his shoe. He pulled it off, but then didn't know where to throw it away. So he jammed it in his jeans pocket.

"If Howie sounds like an orchestra, and we sound like three guitars and a kiddie keyboard, we're in major trouble," Lily warned.

"It's *not* a kiddie keyboard!" Jared protested.

I laughed. "Just because you wind a crank at the side of it doesn't make it a kiddie keyboard!"

"It's small — but it has all the notes," Jared insisted. He set the keyboard on the coffee table and bent down to plug it in.

"Let's stop messing around and get to work," Kristina said, moving her fingers over the frets of her shiny red Gibson. "What song do you want to practice first?"

"How can we practice without Manny?" I asked. "I mean, what's the point?"

"I tried calling him," Lily said. "But his phone is messed up or something. It didn't even ring."

"Let's go to his house and get him," I suggested.

"Yeah. Good idea!" Kristina agreed.

All four of us started for the front entryway to get our coats. But Lily stopped at the door. "Larry and I will go," she announced to Kristina. "You and Jared should stay and practice. Why should we all go?"

"Okay," Jared agreed quickly. "Besides, someone should be here in case Manny shows up."

With that settled, Lily and I pulled on our coats

and headed out the front door. Lily's Doc Martens splashed through a wide puddle as we made our way along the sidewalk.

"I hate it when the snow gets all gray and slushy," she said. "Listen. All you can hear is dripping. Water dripping from the trees, dripping from the houses."

She stuck out her arm to block my path and stop me from walking. We listened in silence to the dripping sounds.

"It's deafening — isn't it?" Lily asked, smiling. The sunlight reflected in her eyes. One blue eye, one green eye.

"Deafening," I repeated. Lily can be pretty weird sometimes. She once told me that she writes poetry. Long poems about nature. But she's never shown any of them to me.

We trudged through the slush. The sun felt warm on my face. I unzipped my parka.

Manny's house came into view as we turned the corner. Manny lives in a square-shaped brick house on top of a hill. It's a great sledding hill. There were two little kids sledding down it now on blue plastic discs. They were going pretty slow since most of the snow had melted.

We walked past them and made our way up to Manny's front stoop. Lily rang the doorbell, and I knocked. "Hey, Manny — open up!" I shouted.

No reply.

No sounds at all. Just the *drip drip drip* of water from the gutter.

"Hey, Manny!" I called. We rang and knocked again.

"No one home," Lily said quietly. She stepped off the stoop and moved to the front window. Edging up on tiptoes, she tried to peer in.

"See anything?" I called.

She shook her head. "No. The sun is reflecting on the glass. It looks dark inside."

"There's no car in the driveway," I said. I knocked one more time, as hard as I could. To my surprise, the front door swung in a little.

"Hey — the door is open!" I called to Lily. She hurried back to the stoop. I pushed the door open a little further. "Anyone home?" I called in.

No reply.

"Hey — your door is open!" I shouted.

Lily pushed the door all the way, and we stepped inside. "Manny?" she called, cupping her hands around her mouth. "Manny?"

I stepped into the living room — and gasped.

I tried to speak. But I couldn't. I couldn't believe what I saw.

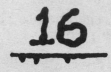

## 16

Lily grabbed my arm as we both stared around the living room.

The room was totally bare. No furniture. No curtains. No paintings or posters on the wall. Even the carpet had been removed, leaving shiny dark floorboards.

"Wh-where did they go?" I managed to choke out.

Lily made her way through the back hall to the kitchen. Also empty. Everything gone. An empty hole where the refrigerator had stood.

"They moved!" Lily exclaimed. "I don't believe it!"

"But why didn't Manny tell us?" I demanded, my eyes moving around the deserted room. "Why didn't he tell us his family was moving away?"

Lily shook her head and didn't reply. The house was silent. I could hear water dripping from the gutter outside.

"Maybe they had to move suddenly," Lily said finally.

"Suddenly? Why?" I demanded.

It was a question that neither of us could answer.

I love to run.

Not when I'm running from snarling dogs. But I do love to run.

I like the way it gets my heart pounding. And I like the *thud* of my sneakers on the ground, and the feeling of my muscles all working together.

On Saturday mornings I like to go jogging with my dad. He always jogs at Miller Woods, along a path that curves around a small lake.

It's really pretty there. The air is always fresh-smelling. And it's a very quiet place.

Dad is tall and lean and pretty athletic. He used to be blond like me, but now his hair is mostly gray, and he has a big bald spot on top.

He jogs every morning before work. I think he usually jogs pretty fast. But on Saturdays, he slows down so that we can run side by side.

We usually jog without talking. That way we can concentrate on the scenery and the fresh air.

But this Saturday morning, I felt like talking. I had decided to tell Dad everything. About the bottle of INSTA-TAN. And about the black hair that kept sprouting.

As I talked, I kept my eyes straight ahead. I saw two big crows float down from the clear blue sky and perch side by side on the bare limb of a tree. The crows cawed loudly, as if talking to us.

The lake sparkled brightly as Dad and I followed the curving path around it. Small patches of ice bobbed in the blue-green water.

I started at the beginning and told the whole story. Dad slowed down a little more to listen. But we kept jogging as I talked.

I told him about finding the bottle of tanning lotion and how we all splashed it on ourselves as a joke. Dad nodded but kept his eyes straight ahead. "I guess it didn't work," he said, sounding a little breathless from running. "You don't look too tan, Larry."

"No, it didn't work," I continued. "The bottle was really old, Dad. It had expired a long time ago."

I took a deep breath. The next part was the hardest to tell. "It didn't give me a tan, Dad. But something really weird started happening to me."

He kept jogging. We both leaped over a fallen tree branch. I slipped over a pile of wet leaves, but quickly caught my balance.

"This weird hair started growing on me," I told him in a shaky voice. "First on the back of my hand. Then on both hands. Then on my knees."

Dad stopped. He turned to me with a worried expression on his face. "Hair?"

I nodded, breathing hard. "Black hair. Thick clumps of it. Very rough and spikey."

Dad swallowed hard. His eyes grew wide. With surprise? With fear? With disbelief?

I couldn't tell.

But to my surprise, he grabbed my arm and started to pull me. "Come on, Larry. We've got to go."

"But, Dad — " I started, holding back.

He tightened his grip and pulled harder. "I *said* we've got to *go!*" he insisted through gritted teeth. "Now!"

He tugged so hard, he nearly pulled me off my feet!

"Dad — what's wrong?" I demanded in a high, shrill voice. "What is it?"

He didn't answer. He pulled me back along the path toward the street. His eyes were wild. His whole face was twisted into a tight, frightened scowl.

"Dad — what's wrong?" I cried. "Where are you taking me? Where?"

# 17

Dr. Murkin raised the hypodermic needle and examined it in the light. "Turn away, Larry," he said softly. "I know you don't like to watch. This won't hurt at all."

Pain shot through my arm as the needle sank in. I shut my eyes and held my breath until he pulled out the needle.

"I know it's early," he said, rubbing my arm with a cotton ball dipped in alcohol. "But since you were here, I thought I'd give you your shot."

My dad sat tensely in a folding chair against the wall of the small examining room. He had his arms crossed tightly over the front of his sweatshirt.

"Wh-what about the hair?" I stammered to Dr. Murkin. "Did the INSTA-TAN — "

The doctor shook his head. "I really don't think tanning lotion can cause hair to grow, Larry. Those lotions work on the pigments of the skin. They — "

"But it was a very old bottle!" I insisted.

"Maybe the ingredients turned sour or something!"

He waved his hand, as if to say, "No way."

Then he turned and started scribbling notes in my file. "I'm sorry, Larry," he said, writing rapidly in a tiny handwriting. "It wasn't the tanning lotion. Trust me."

He turned his head to me, his eyes studying me. "I've examined you from head to foot. You passed every test. You seem fine to me."

"Whew! That's a relief!" Dad said, sighing.

"But the hair — !" I insisted.

"Let's wait and see," Dr. Murkin replied, his eyes on my dad.

"Wait and see?" I cried. "You're not going to give me any medicine or anything to stop it?"

"Maybe it won't happen again," Dr. Murkin said. He closed my file. Then he motioned for me to jump down from the examining table.

"Try not to worry, Larry," he said, handing my coat to me. "You'll be okay."

"Thank you, Dr. Murkin," Dad said, climbing to his feet. He flashed the doctor a smile, but I could see that it was forced. Dad still looked really tense.

I followed Dad out to the parking lot. We didn't say anything until we were in the car and on the way home. "Feel better?" Dad asked, his eyes narrowed straight ahead on the road.

"No," I replied glumly.

"What's wrong?" Dad asked impatiently. "Dr. Murkin said you checked out fine."

"What about the ugly black hair?" I demanded angrily. "What about it? Why didn't he do anything about it? Do you think he didn't believe me?"

"I'm sure he believed you," Dad said softly.

"Then why didn't he do anything to help me?" I wailed.

Dad didn't reply for the longest time. He stared straight through the windshield, chewing his lower lip. Then, finally, he said in a hushed voice, "Sometimes the best thing is to wait."


We met at Lily's house for band practice that afternoon. We sounded pretty good — but it wasn't the same without Manny.

We were all really upset that he had moved away without saying good-bye. Lily asked her mom to call some friends who were friendly with Manny's parents. She wanted to find out where Manny and his family had moved.

But the friends turned out to be as surprised as we were.

We couldn't find anyone who knew that Manny's family planned to move from our town.

I have to admit that our songs sounded better with two guitars instead of three. Lily has a very light singing voice — not much power. And three guitars nearly always drowned her out.

With Manny gone, we could actually hear Lily some of the time.

I kept messing up the Beatles song we were rehearsing — "I Want to Hold Your Hand." I played the wrong chords and couldn't get the rhythm right.

I knew what the trouble was. I couldn't stop thinking about Dr. Murkin and how he didn't believe me about the hair. He said it wasn't the INSTA-TAN. But maybe he was wrong.

I felt so angry — and so . . . alone.

Glancing around Lily's living room as we started "I Want to Hold Your Hand" for the twentieth time, I studied my friends. Were they having the same problem? Were they growing ugly, black hair, too, and afraid to tell anyone?

The first time I had asked, Lily had laughed at me and called me Hairy Larry. But I had to ask again. I couldn't think about anything else. I had to know the truth.

I waited till practice was over. Kristina was tucking her guitar into its case. Jared went into the kitchen to get a Coke from the fridge. Lily was standing beside the couch, one hand twirling the gold pirate coin at her throat.

"I — I have to ask you something," I said nervously when Jared returned to the room.

He popped the top on the can, and a spray of Coke hit him in the face.

Everyone laughed.

"Can't you work a Coke can?" Lily joked. "Do you need an instruction book?"

"Ha-ha," Jared replied sarcastically, wiping his face with his sleeve. "You deliberately shook the cans, Lily, so people would get squirted. Admit it."

Kristina laughed as she snapped her guitar case shut. "Maybe you should stick to juice boxes, Jared."

He stuck out his tongue at her.

I cleared my throat loudly. "I want to ask you guys something," I repeated in a shaky voice.

They were all in a great mood, laughing and kidding around. They all seemed totally normal.

Why was I the only one who felt worried and afraid?

"Remember the INSTA-TAN stuff?" I started. "Have any of you been growing hair since we put that stuff on?" I could feel my face turning red. "I mean, really ugly patches of black hair?"

Jared started to laugh, and Coke spurted out of his nose. He started to choke. Kristina hurried over to slap him on the back.

"Hairy Larry!" Jared cried when he stopped choking. He pointed the Coke can at me and started chanting. "Hairy Larry! Hairy Larry!"

"Come on, guys!" I pleaded. "I'm serious!"

That made Kristina and Jared laugh even harder.

I turned to Lily, who was still standing beside the couch. She had a troubled expression on her face. She definitely wasn't laughing. She lowered her eyes to the floor as I continued to stare at her.

"Larry is a werewolf!" Jared declared.

"I hope The Geeks don't have to play when there's a full moon!" Kristina exclaimed.

"Maybe Larry's howling is better than his guitar playing!" Jared said. They both laughed.

"I — I was just making a joke!" I stammered. I wanted a hole to open up in the floor so that I could disappear into it.

*I'm the only one*, I realized. *I'm the only one who is growing the ugly hair.*

That's why Jared and Kristina thought it was so funny. It wasn't happening to them. They didn't have to worry about it.

But Lily wasn't joining in with the jokes. She turned away and started picking up music sheets from the floor and straightening the room.

Lily always enjoys teasing me and making me blush. I stared at her, wondering if she had the same secret I did.

I packed up my guitar slowly and waited for Jared and Kristina to leave. Then I put on my coat and baseball cap and followed Lily to the front door.

On the front stoop, I turned back to her. "Lily, tell me the truth," I insisted, studying her face. "Have you been growing weird patches of black hair on your hands and knees?"

She hesitated, chewing her bottom lip. "I . . . I don't want to talk about it," she replied in a whisper.

Then she slammed the front door.

I didn't move from the concrete stoop. I kept picturing her troubled expression. I kept hearing her whispered voice.

Was it happening to Lily? If it was, why wouldn't she admit it to me? Was she too embarrassed?

Or was she embarrassed for *me*?

Maybe it wasn't happening to her, I realized. Maybe she just thinks I'm crazy. Maybe she feels bad for me because I keep acting like such a jerk.

Feeling totally confused, I turned and headed for the street. The sun was still high in the sky, but the air felt cold. A sharp wind blew at my face as I started toward home.

Leaning into the wind, I reached up and tugged down my cap to keep it from blowing away. To my surprise, I couldn't pull it down.

The cap suddenly felt tight. Too tight.

I removed it and held it close to my face to study it. Had someone adjusted the back to make it tighter?

No.

A chill of dread ran down my back as I raised a hand to my forehead. And discovered why my cap didn't fit.

My entire forehead was covered with thick, bristly hair.

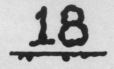

## 18

I burst through the back door, into the kitchen. "Mom — look at this!" I cried. "Look at my head!"

My eyes darted around the room. "Mom?"

Not there.

I ran through the house, calling for her. I decided it was time to show my parents what was happening to me. Time to make them believe me.

The stripe of hair would totally gross them out, would finally convince them this was *serious*.

"Mom! Dad? Anybody home?"

No.

When I returned to the kitchen, I found a note on the refrigerator: *WE WENT SHOPPING IN BROOKESDALE VILLAGE. HOME LATE. FIX YOURSELF A SNACK.*

With a cry of disgust, I tossed my cap across the room. Then I pulled off my parka and let it fall to the floor.

My heart pounding, I made my way to the mirror in the front hall and studied myself. I looked like some kind of comic book mutant!

My pale face stared back at me. It appeared exactly the same. Except that I had a thick, black stripe of fur across my forehead.

Looks like I'm wearing a bandanna, I thought miserably. Like one of those headbands that skiers wear. Except this one is made of disgusting hair.

I ran a trembling hand over the thick hair.

My chest heaved up and down. I felt like crying and screaming furiously at the same time. I felt like grabbing the stripe of fur and ripping it out of my head.

I couldn't bear to look at myself. The hair was so gross, so disgusting.

I decided there was no way I could wait for Mom and Dad to get home. I couldn't leave that horrible hair on my face. Spinning away from the mirror, I ran upstairs to shave it off.

I lathered up the strip of hair with shaving cream. Then I began to scrape my dad's razor over it.

"Ow!" It hurt, but I didn't care. I had to cut it off. Every thick, bristly strand of it.

Watching the hair fall into the sink, I suddenly knew what I had to do. I had to find the INSTA-TAN bottle. I had to find it and take it to Dr. Murkin.

"If I bring him the bottle, I can make him believe me!" I told myself. Then Dr. Murkin can do tests on it. He can figure out why it's making hair grow on me.

And once he knows that it's the INSTA-TAN that's growing hair, Dr. Murkin will give me a cure, I decided.

But where did we toss the bottle?

I shut my eyes and struggled to remember.

After I discovered the bottle, we had all run into Lily's house to splash the stuff on. Then we had gone back outside to mess around in the snow.

Did we toss the INSTA-TAN bottle back in the trash Dumpster next door?

I had to find out.

I scribbled a note to my parents, telling them I left something at Lily's and would be back soon. Then I grabbed my coat and hurried out the door.

The air had become a lot colder. Clouds had rolled over the sun, making the evening sky gray. I zipped up my parka and pulled the hood over my head. My forehead still tingled from where I had shaved it.

The three blocks to Lily's house seemed like three miles! As I turned the corner, her house came into view.

I don't want her to see me, I realized. If she sees me poking around that trash Dumpster, she'll want to know why. And I'm not ready to tell her the whole story.

She wouldn't tell *me* the truth, I thought bitterly. Instead, she slammed the door on me.

So I'm not ready to tell her the truth, either.

I felt glad that it had become so dark out. Maybe Lily wouldn't see me.

I kept my eyes on her house as I approached. The lights were on in the dining room. Maybe her family was having an early dinner.

Good, I thought. I'll dig into the trash Dumpster, pull out the bottle, and disappear before they finish, before anyone has a chance to glance out the window.

I stopped short when I saw that there was just one little problem.

The trash Dumpster was gone.

The workers must have hauled it away.

I let out a long sigh and nearly slumped to my knees. "Now what?" I murmured out loud.

Now how do I prove to Dr. Murkin that the INSTA-TAN is making me grow hair?

The cold wind swirled around me as I stared at the curb where the Dumpster had stood. Fat brown leaves, blown by the twisting wind, fluttered around my legs.

I shivered.

Turning to leave, a memory flashed through my mind.

The INSTA-TAN bottle. We *hadn't* dropped it back into the Dumpster. We had tossed it into the woods on the other side of the neighbors' house.

"Yes!" I cried happily. "Yes!"

We had chased each other across the neighbors' yard — and I'd heaved the bottle into the trees.

It will still be there, I told myself. It *has* to be there.

I darted past Lily's house, glancing up at the front windows. I couldn't see anyone looking out.

Past the neighbors' house, dark and empty. The remodeling work not finished.

Into the woods. The dead leaves wet and slippery under my shoes. The bare tree branches shook and rattled in the shifting, sharp wind.

Where had the bottle landed? I asked myself. Where?

It hadn't gone far, I remembered. Just past the first trees.

It had to be nearby, I knew. Somewhere near where I stood.

A blanket of deep shadow had fallen over the woods. I kicked at a pile of dead leaves. My shoe hit something hard.

Bending quickly, I tossed leaves away with both hands.

Only a tree branch.

I moved deeper into the woods, pushing my way through clumps of tall, dead weeds.

I stopped.

It has to be around here, I knew. My eyes desperately searched the shadows.

There it is. No. Just a smooth stone.

I kicked it away. Then I turned slowly, making a complete circle, my eyes sweeping the dark ground.

Where is the bottle? Where?

I sucked in my breath when I heard the sound.

The crack of a twig.

I listened hard. I heard the crackle of leaves. The brush of a leg against a winter-dry shrub.

Another twig cracking.

Swallowing hard, I realized I was no longer alone.

"Wh-who's there?" I called.

# 19

"Who's there?"

No reply.

Frozen as still as a statue, I listened. I heard the scrape of feet moving rapidly over the ground. I heard heavy breathing.

"Hey — who is it?" I called.

I glanced down — and saw the bottle. Lying on its side, nestled in a pile of leaves right in front of me.

I bent quickly, reached eagerly for the bottle with both hands. But I jerked back up to my feet in fright as a dark figure lumbered out from the trees.

Panting hard. Its long tongue flapping from its open mouth.

A tall, brown dog. Even in the dim light, I could see how scraggly and tangled its fur was. I could see large burrs stuck in its heaving side.

I took a step back. "Are you alone, boy?" I called

in a frightened whisper. "Huh? Are you alone, doggie?"

The animal lowered its head and let out a whimper.

I searched the woods for other dogs. Was he part of a pack? Part of the pack of stray dogs that liked to chase me, growling and snapping?

I didn't see any others.

"Good dog," I told him, keeping my voice low and calm. "Good doggie."

He stared up at me, still panting. His scraggly, brown tail wagged once, then drooped.

I bent slowly, keeping my eyes on the dog, and picked up the bottle. It felt surprisingly cold. I held it up and tried to see if any of the liquid remained inside.

But it was too dark to see.

I'm pretty sure I didn't use every last drop, I thought, struggling to remember. There has to be a little left. Enough for Dr. Murkin to test.

I shook the bottle close to my ear, listening for the splash of liquid inside. *Please, please, let there be a drop left!* I pleaded silently.

The trees shivered in a sharp, swirling gust. Leaves rustled and scraped against each other.

The dog let out another soft whimper.

I grasped the bottle tightly in my right hand and started to back away. "Bye-bye, doggie."

He tilted his head and stared up at me.

I took another step back. "Bye, doggie," I repeated softly. "Go home. Go home, boy."

He didn't move. He let out another whimper. Then his tail began to wag.

I took another step back, grasping the INSTA-TAN bottle tightly. Then, as I started to turn away from the staring dog, I saw the others.

They poked out quickly, silently, from the dark trees. Five or six big dogs, their eyes glowing angrily. Then five or six more.

As they lumbered nearer, moving quickly, steadily, I could hear their growls, low and menacing. They pulled back their lips and bared their teeth.

I froze, staring in terror at their darkly glowing eyes, listening to their menacing, low growls.

Then I spun around awkwardly. Started to run.

"Ohh!" I let out a shrill cry as I stumbled over a fallen tree branch.

The bottle flew out of my hand.

As I fell, I reached out for it, grasping desperately.

Missed.

I watched in horror as it hit a sharp rock — and shattered. The jagged pieces flew in all directions. A tiny puddle of brown liquid washed over the rock.

I landed hard on my knees and elbows. Pain shot through my body. But I ignored it and scrambled to my feet.

I whirled around to face the dogs.

But to my surprise, they were running in a different direction. Through the trees, I glimpsed a frightened rabbit, scrabbling over the leafy ground. Barking and growling, the dogs chased after it.

My heart pounding, my knees still throbbing, I walked over to the rock and stared down at the jagged pieces of orange glass. I picked one up and examined it closely.

"*Now* what do I do?" I asked myself out loud. I could still hear the excited barking of the dogs in the distance. "Now what?"

The bottle was shattered into a dozen pieces. My evidence was gone. I had nothing to show Dr. Murkin. Nothing at all.

With an angry cry, I tossed the piece of glass at the trees. Then I wearily slunk toward home.

Mom and Dad hurried to a school meeting after dinner. I went upstairs to my room to do my homework.

I didn't feel like being alone.

I took Jasper in my lap and petted her for a while. But she wasn't in the mood. She glared at me with those weird yellow eyes. When that didn't work, she scratched my hand, jumped away, and disappeared out of the room.

I tried calling Lily, but no one answered at her place.

Outside, the wind howled around the corner of the house. It made my bedroom windows rattle.

A chill ran down my back.

I leaned my elbows on my desk and hunched over my government textbook. But I couldn't concentrate. The words on the page became a gray blur.

I walked across the room and picked up my guitar. Then I bent down and plugged it into my amp.

Lots of times when I'm feeling nervous or upset, I play my guitar for a while. It always calms me down.

I cranked the amp up really high and started to play a loud blues melody. There was no one else home, no one to tell me to turn it down. I wanted to play as loud as I could — loud enough to drown out my troubled thoughts.

But I had played for only three or four minutes when I realized that something was wrong.

I kept missing notes. Messing up the chords.

What's wrong with me? I wondered. I've played this tune a million times. I can play it in my sleep.

When I glanced down at my fingers, I saw the problem.

"Ohh!" I uttered a weak groan. That disgusting hair had sprouted over both of my hands. My fingers were covered in thick, black hair.

I turned my hands over. Both palms were covered, too.

The guitar fell heavily to the floor as I jumped to my feet.

My arms began to itch.

With trembling hands, I tore at the cuffs. Pulled up the sleeves.

My arms were covered, too! The thick, bristly hair swept over both arms and hands.

I stood there, swallowing hard, staring down at my hairy arms and hands. My legs were trembling. I felt weak.

My mouth suddenly felt dry. My throat ached. I tried to swallow.

Was the disgusting hair growing on my *tongue*?

Feeling a jolt of nausea, I lurched across the hall to the bathroom. Clicking on the ceiling light, I leaned over the sink. I brought my face up close to the mirror and stuck out my tongue.

No.

My tongue was okay.

But my face — my cheeks and chin — were covered with black hair.

It's spreading so fast! I realized. The mirror reflected my horror.

It's spreading so fast now — all over me.

What am I going to do?

Isn't there *anything* I can do?

I got to school early on Monday morning and waited for Lily at her locker.

It had taken hours to shave off all the bristly clumps of hair. But I did it.

This morning I wore a sweater with extra-long sleeves, and I pulled a baseball cap down low on my head in case the hair grew back during the day.

"Lily, where are you?" I murmured impatiently. I paced nervously back and forth in front of the row of green lockers.

Lily and I have to face this problem together, I told myself. I remembered the frightened expression on Lily's face when I asked her if she had been growing weird hair.

I *knew* the same thing was happening to Lily. I just knew it.

And I knew that Lily must be embarrassed like me, too embarrassed to admit it, to talk about it.

But the two of us can figure out what to do, I decided.

If the two of us go to Dr. Murkin and tell him about the INSTA-TAN lotion and the hair, he'll *have* to believe us.

But where was Lily?

Kids jammed the hall, slamming lockers, laughing and talking. I glanced at my watch. Only three minutes till the bell rang.

"How's it going, Larry?" a voice called.

I turned and saw Howie Hurwin grinning at me. His sister, Marissa, stood beside him. Her braid was caught in her backpack strap, and she was struggling to free it.

"Hi, Howie," I said, sighing. He was the *last* person I wanted to see this morning!

"Ready for tomorrow?" he asked. Why did he have to grin like that when he talked? That grin just made me want to punch him.

"Tomorrow?" I glanced down the crowded hall, searching for Lily.

Howie laughed. "Did you forget about the Battle of the Bands?"

"Ow!" Marissa cried. She finally managed to tug her braid free. "Is your band still going to play?" she asked. "We heard about Manny leaving."

"Yeah. We'll be there," I told her. "We sound pretty good."

"We do, too!" Howie replied, grinning even

wider. "We might be on TV. My uncle knows a woman who works on *Star Search*. He thinks maybe he can get us on."

"Great," I replied, without any enthusiasm.

Where was Lily?

"If we get on that show, we'll probably win," Marissa added, still fiddling with her long braid. "And then we'll be famous."

"They asked us to play at the next school dance," Howie said. "They didn't ask *your* band, did they?"

"No," I replied. "No one asked us."

That made Howie's grin practically burst off his face. "Too bad," he said.

The bell rang. "I've got to go," I said, hurrying toward Miss Shindling's room.

"See you at the contest tomorrow," Marissa called.

"We're going first," Howie shouted. "I guess they're saving the best for *first*!"

I heard the two of them laughing as I stepped into the classroom. I made my way to my seat, searching for Lily. Had she slipped past me while I was talking with Howie and Marissa?

No. No sign of her.

I sank into my seat, feeling worried and disappointed. Was Lily sick today? I hoped not. She can't get sick the day before the Battle of the Bands, I told myself. She just can't.

"Larry, would you hand out the tests?" Miss Shindling asked, dropping a heavy stack of papers into my arms.

"Huh? Test?"

I had totally forgotten.

Lily didn't come to school. I tried phoning her at lunchtime. The phone rang and rang, but no one answered.

After school, I decided to go to Lily's house to see what had happened to her. But as I walked out of the school building, I remembered that my mom had asked me to come straight home after school. She had some chores she wanted me to help her with.

It was a clear, cold day. Puffy, white clouds floated high in the afternoon sky. All the snow had finally melted, but the ground was still soft and wet.

I waited for several cars to pass. Then I crossed the street and headed for home.

I had walked nearly a block when I realized I was being followed.

A dog brushed softly against my leg. Startled, I stopped and stared down at it.

The dog had light brown fur, almost red, with a white patch at its throat. It was a medium-sized dog, a little bigger than a cocker spaniel. It had long, floppy brown ears and a long, furry tail that swept slowly back and forth as it gazed up at me.

"Who are you?" I asked it. "I've never seen *you* before."

I glanced around, making sure there weren't a dozen other dogs lurking in the bushes, getting ready to chase after me.

Then I turned and started walking again.

The dog brushed my leg again and kept on going. As I walked, it stayed a few yards ahead of me, glancing back to make sure I was following.

"Are you following *me* — or am I following *you*?" I called to it.

The dog's tail gave a single wag in reply.

It followed me all the way home.

My mom was waiting for me in the driveway. She had a long green sweater pulled down over her jeans. "Nice day," she commented, glancing up at the sunny sky.

"Hi, Mom," I greeted her. "This dog followed me home."

The dog sniffed at the low evergreen shrubs that lined the front walk.

"She's kind of pretty," Mom said. "What a nice color. Who does she belong to?"

I shrugged. "Beats me. I've never seen her before."

The dog came over and stared up at Mom.

"At least she's friendly," I said, setting my heavy backpack down on the driveway. "Maybe we should keep her."

"No way," Mom replied sharply. "No dogs. Not with Jasper in the house."

I bent down and petted the top of the dog's head.

"She has a tag on her collar," Mom said, pointing. "Check it out, Larry. Maybe it says the owner's name."

The dog's tail wagged furiously as I petted her head. "Good dog," I said softly.

"Come on, Larry. See what the tag says," Mom insisted.

"Okay, okay." I reached for the round, gold tag hanging down from the dog's collar. Then I dropped to my knees and lowered my face so that I could see it clearly.

"Huh?"

I recognized it instantly.

It wasn't a dog tag. It was Lily's gold pirate coin.

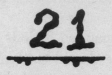

# 21

I nearly fell over. I felt as if someone had kicked me in the stomach.

"M-mom!" I stammered. But my voice came out as a gasp.

"Larry — what are you doing?" Mom called. She had wandered to the side of the driveway and was pulling up some dead weeds. "What does the tag say?"

"It — it isn't a tag," I finally managed to choke out.

She turned her head back to me. "Huh?"

"It isn't a dog tag," I repeated, still holding it between my fingers. "It's Lily's gold pirate coin."

Mom laughed. "Why would Lily give her coin to a dog? Didn't her grandfather give her that coin?"

"I — I don't know why," I stammered. "I don't get it, Mom."

The dog's hot breath brushed over my hand. She pulled away from me, settled back, and started scratching her long, floppy ear with her back paw.

"Are you sure it's a gold coin, Larry?" Mom asked, crossing the drive, standing right behind me.

I nodded and reached for the coin again. "Yeah. It's Lily's gold coin, Mom."

"It must be some *other* gold coin," Mom suggested. "I'm sure it isn't the same coin."

Mom must be right, I decided.

I let go of the coin and raised my hand to pet the dog's head.

But my hand stopped in midair when I saw the dog's eyes.

She had one blue eye and one green eye.

# 22

"It's Lily! It's Lily!" I shrieked, jumping to my feet.

My shouts frightened the dog. She uttered a shrill *yip*, turned, and bolted from the front yard.

"Lily — come back!" I called after her. "Come back! Lily!"

"Larry — wait!" Mom cried. "Please — !"

I didn't hear the rest of what she said. Jumping over my backpack, I darted toward the street. I hurtled across without slowing to look for cars — and kept running toward Lily's house.

It *is* Lily! I told myself. That dog has a green eye and a blue eye. And it's wearing Lily's coin!

It *is* Lily! I *know* it!

I could hear my mom calling for me to come back. But I ignored her and kept running.

Lily's house was three blocks away. I ran at full speed the whole way. By the time her house came into view, I was gasping for breath, and I had a sharp pain in my side.

But I didn't care.

I had to see Lily. I had to know for sure that the dog wasn't Lily.

Such a crazy thought! As I crossed the street, I started to realize how crazy it was.

Lily, a dog?

Larry, are you totally losing it? I asked myself. Mom must think I'm totally wacko! I realized.

Lily, a dog?

I slowed down, rubbing the pain at my side, trying to massage it away.

I spotted Lily's parents in the driveway. The trunk of their blue Chevy was open. Mr. Vonn was lifting a suitcase into it.

"Hi!" I called breathlessly. "Hey — hi!"

"Hello, Larry," Mrs. Vonn said as I stepped up to the car. I saw two other suitcases and some smaller bags waiting to be loaded into the car.

"Going on a trip?" I asked, struggling to catch my breath. The pain in my side kept throbbing, refusing to go away.

They didn't answer. Mr. Vonn groaned as he hoisted a heavy suitcase into the trunk.

"Where's Lily?" I asked. I handed him one of the smaller bags. "She wasn't in school today."

"We're going away," Mrs. Vonn said quietly from behind me.

"Well, where's Lily?" I repeated. "Is she inside?"

Mr. Vonn frowned, but didn't reply.

I turned to Lily's mom. "Can I see her?" I asked impatiently. "Is Lily inside?"

"You must have the wrong house," she replied softly.

My mouth dropped open. "Wrong house? Mrs. Vonn — what do you mean?"

"There's no one here named Lily," she said.

## 23

For some reason, I burst out laughing.

Startled laughter. Frightened laughter.

Mrs. Vonn's sad expression cut my laughter short — and sent a chill down my back.

"Is Lily — ?" I started to say.

Mrs. Vonn grabbed my shoulder and squeezed it. She lowered her face close to mine. "Listen to what I'm telling you, Larry," she said through gritted teeth.

"But — but — " I sputtered.

"There *is* no Lily," she repeated, squeezing my shoulder hard. "Just forget about her." She had tears in her eyes.

Mr. Vonn slammed the car trunk. I jumped out of Mrs. Vonn's grasp, my heart pounding.

"You'd better go," Mr. Vonn said firmly, coming over to join his wife.

I took a step back. My legs felt weak and shaky.

"But, Lily — " I started.

"You'd better go," Mr. Vonn repeated.

At the side of the garage, I spotted the red-brown dog. She whimpered sadly, her head hung low.

I whirled around and ran, as fast as I could.

Mom and Dad acted so strange at dinner. They refused to discuss Lily or the dog or Lily's parents.

Mom and Dad kept glancing at each other, giving each other meaningful looks that I wasn't supposed to see.

They think I'm crazy! I realized. That's why they're refusing to talk about it. They think I'm losing my mind. They don't want to say anything to me until they decide how they're going to handle me.

"I'm not crazy!" I shouted suddenly, dropping my fork and knife onto the table. I hadn't touched my spaghetti and meatballs.

How could I eat?

"I'm not crazy! I'm not making this up!"

"Can't we talk about it another time?" Mom pleaded, glancing at Dad.

"Let's just finish our dinner," Dad added, keeping his eyes on his plate.

After dinner, I called Jared and Kristina over to give them the bad news. I didn't want them to think that I was crazy. So I simply told them that Lily had gone away.

"But what about tomorrow?" Jared cried.

"Yeah. What about the Battle of the Bands?" Kristina demanded. "How could Lily leave on the day before the contest?"

I shrugged. We were sitting in the living room. Kristina and I sat on opposite ends of the couch. Jared was sprawled in the chair across from me.

Jasper brushed over my feet. I leaned down and lifted her into my lap. Her yellow eyes stared up at me. Then she closed them and settled against me, purring softly.

"Where did Lily go?" Kristina asked angrily, drumming her fingers on the couch arm. "On vacation? Why didn't she tell us she was going to miss the contest?"

"Howie Hurwin will jump for joy when he hears this news," Jared muttered glumly, shaking his head.

"I don't know where Lily went," I told them. "I saw her parents loading suitcases into the car. Now they're gone. That's all I know. I'm sure Lily is very unhappy. I know Lily wanted to be with us. I don't think she had a choice."

I had a sudden urge to tell them everything that had happened. But I didn't want them to start laughing at me. Or worrying about me.

I felt so mixed up. I didn't know what I wanted to do.

I wanted Lily back. And Manny. That I knew.

And I wanted the ugly hair to stop sprouting all over my body.

107

If only I had never found that bottle of INSTA-TAN.

This was all my fault. All of it.

"So I guess The Geeks have to pull out of the band contest tomorrow," I said glumly.

"I guess," Jared repeated, shaking his head.

"No way!" Kristina cried, surprising both of us. She jumped to her feet and stood between Jared and me. She balled both hands into fists. "No way!" she repeated.

"But we don't have a singer — " Jared protested.

"I can sing," Kristina replied quickly. "I'm a pretty good singer."

"But you haven't rehearsed any of the songs," Jared said. "Do you know the words?"

Kristina nodded. "All of them."

"But, Kristina — " I started.

"Listen, guys," she said sharply, "we *have* to go onstage tomorrow. Even if it's just the three of us. We can't let Howie Hurwin win tomorrow — can we?"

"I'd like to wipe that grin off Howie's face," I muttered.

"Me, too," Jared agreed. "But how can we? Two guitars and a keyboard? Howie has his full band. He'll blast us out of the auditorium."

"Not if we play our hearts out!" Kristina exclaimed with emotion. "Not if we give it our best."

"Let's do it for Lily!" I blurted out. The words

just tumbled from my mouth. As soon as I said it, I felt embarrassed.

But Kristina and Jared picked right up on it. "Let's do it for Lily!" they both cried. "We can win! We really can! Let's win it for Lily!"

So it was decided. The Geeks would go onstage tomorrow afternoon. Could we win? Could we beat Howie and the Shouters?

Probably not.

But we'd give it our best shot.

"Let's go up to my room and practice a little," I suggested.

Jared started toward the stairs. But Kristina didn't move.

I turned and found her staring at my face in horror.

"Larry — !" she cried, pointing. "What's *that* on your forehead?"

# 24

I gasped in horror.

My hand shot up to my forehead.

The ugly black hair — it had grown back, I knew. And now Kristina and Jared were both staring at it. They both saw it — saw that I was becoming some kind of hairy monster.

I rubbed my forehead with a trembling hand. Smooth.

My forehead was smooth!

"It's right there." Kristina pointed.

I hurried over to the hallway mirror and gazed up at my forehead. I discovered an orange smear near my right temple.

"It's spaghetti sauce," I moaned. "I must have rubbed my face during dinner."

I rubbed off the orange spot. My entire body was shaking. Kristina had scared me to death! Over a dumb spot of spaghetti sauce!

"Larry, are you okay?" she asked, standing behind me and staring at my reflection in the mirror. "You look kind of weird."

"I'm okay," I replied quickly, trying to force my body to stop shaking and quaking.

"Hey — don't get sick," Jared warned. "Kristina and I can't go on the stage by ourselves tomorrow."

"I'll be there," I told them. "Don't worry, guys. I'll be there."

The next afternoon, the whole school jammed into the auditorium to watch the Battle of the Bands.

Feeling really nervous, I stood backstage and peeked out through the curtain. The lights in the auditorium were all on, and Mr. Fosburg, the principal, stood in front of the curtain, both arms raised, trying to get everyone quiet.

Behind me, Howie Hurwin and his band were tuning up, adjusting the amps, making sure the sound was right. Marissa was wearing a very short, sparkly red dress over black tights. She caught me staring at her and flashed me a smug smile.

The Geeks should have dressed up, I realized, watching Marissa. We didn't even think of it. The three of us were wearing T-shirts and jeans, our normal school clothes.

I turned and gazed at Howie's new synthesizer

keyboard. It was about a mile long, and it had a thousand buttons and dials on it. It made Jared's keyboard look like a baby toy.

Howie caught me staring at it. "Cool, huh?" he called, grinning that gruesome grin of his. "Hey, Larry — after we win the contest, you can have my autograph!"

Howie laughed. So did Marissa and the rest of the Shouters.

I turned and slumped away to join Jared and Kristina at the side of the stage. "We're total losers," I moaned, shaking my head.

"Good attitude, Larry," Jared replied sarcastically.

"Maybe Howie's giant keyboard will blow out all the fuses," I said glumly. "That's our only chance."

Kristina rolled her eyes. "They can't be *that* good," she muttered.

But they were.

The auditorium lights darkened. The curtain slid open. Howie and the Shouters stepped into the red-and-blue stage lights. And began blasting out the old Chuck Berry rock-and-roll song "Johnny B. Goode."

They sounded great. And they looked great.

Marissa's dress sparkled in the light. They had worked out dance moves, and they all danced and moved as they played.

We should have thought of that, I told myself

glumly, watching from the side of the stage. When *we* play, the three of us just stand around — like *geeks!*

The kids in the auditorium went crazy. They all jumped to their feet and began clapping along, moving and dancing.

They stayed on their feet for all four of the Shouters' songs. Each song came louder and faster than the last. The old auditorium rocked and shook so hard, I thought the floor might cave in!

Then, as Howie and Marissa and the others took their bows, the auditorium erupted in wild cheers and shouts of, "More! Moooore! Mooooore!"

So Howie and the Shouters did two more songs.

Jared, Kristina, and I kept casting tense glances at each other as they played. This wasn't doing a whole lot for our confidence!

Finally, Howie and Marissa took several more bows and ran off the stage, waving their fists high above their heads in triumph.

"Your turn!" Howie called to me as he ran past. He grinned. "Hey, Larry — where's the rest of your band?"

I started to reply angrily. But Jared gave me a hard shove, and the three of us moved uncertainly onto the stage.

I bent down and plugged my guitar into the amp. Jared worked quickly to adjust the sound level of his little keyboard.

Howie's giant keyboard had been pushed to the back of the stage. It seemed to stare at us, reminding us how good — and loud — the Shouters had sounded.

Kristina stood tensely at the microphone, her arms crossed in front of her T-shirt. I played a few chords, testing the level of the amp. My hands felt cold and sweaty. They slipped over the strings.

The audience was talking and laughing, restless, waiting for us to start.

"Are we ready?" I whispered to Jared and Kristina. "Let's do 'I Want to Hold Your Hand' first. Then go into the Rolling Stones song."

They nodded.

I took a deep breath and steadied my hands on my guitar.

Jared leaned over the keyboard. Kristina uncrossed her arms and stepped to the microphone, jamming both hands into her jeans pockets.

We started the Beatles song.

Shaky at first. All three of us sang on this one. And the harmony was off.

My guitar was too loud. It was drowning out our voices. I wanted to stop and turn it down. But of course I couldn't.

The audience sat quietly, listening. They didn't jump to their feet and start dancing.

They applauded loudly as we finished the song. But it was polite applause. No loud cheering. No real enthusiasm.

*At least we got through it!* I told myself, wiping my sweaty hands on my jeans legs.

I stepped forward as we started the Rolling Stones song.

I had a really long guitar solo in this number. I was praying I didn't mess up.

I nodded to Jared and Kristina. Kristina grabbed the floor microphone with both hands, leaning close to it. Jared started the song on the keyboard.

I started my solo. Badly. I messed up the first chords.

My heart started to thump. My mouth was suddenly too dry to swallow.

I closed my eyes and tried to shut out everything — to concentrate on my fingers, on the music.

As I played, the audience started to cheer. A few shouts at first. Some scattered applause.

But then the cheering grew louder and louder.

Happily, I opened my eyes. Several kids were on their feet, shouting and laughing.

I bent my knees and let my fingers move over the frets, the pick moving automatically now over the strings.

I was starting to feel good — really good.

The cheers grew louder. I realized that several kids were pointing at me.

What's going on? I wondered.

And I suddenly knew that something was

wrong. The cheers were *too* loud. The laughter was too loud. Too many kids were jumping up and pointing fingers at me.

"Great special effects!" I heard a boy shout from the first row.

"Yeah. Great special effects!"

Huh? I thought. *What* special effects?

It didn't take me long to figure it out.

As Kristina started to sing, I reached my hand up and rubbed it over my face.

I cried out in horror as I felt the stiff, prickly hair.

My face was covered in it. My chin, my cheeks, my forehead.

The thick, black hair had sprouted over my entire face.

And the whole school was staring at it, staring at me.

The whole school knew my horrible, embarrassing secret.

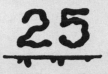

## 25

"We won! We won!"

I heard Jared and Kristina shouting gleefully behind me.

But I set my guitar on the stage floor, turned away from them, and started to run.

The kids in the auditorium were still shouting and cheering.

We had won the contest because of my amazing hairy transformation. "Great special effects!" that kid had shouted. The "special effects" had won the day.

But I wasn't feeling like a winner.

I felt like an ugly freak.

The bushy hair had covered my face, then spread down to my neck and shoulders. Both hands were covered in bristly fur, and I could feel it growing up my arms. My back began to itch. Was it growing on my back, too?

"Hey, Larry — Larry!" I heard Kristina and

Jared calling. "The trophy! Come get your trophy!"

But I was out the stage door, the wild cheers of the audience ringing in my ears. Out the back door of the school. Into a chilly, gray afternoon. Dark clouds low over the trees.

Running now. Running blindly, my heart thudding.

Running home. Covered in thick, black fur.

Running in panic, in shame. In fear.

The houses and trees passed in a gray blur. As I turned up my driveway, I saw Mom and Dad back by the garage. They both turned to me, surprise on their faces.

"Look at me!" I shrieked. "Look!" My voice burst out, hoarse and terrified. "Now do you believe me?"

They gaped at me, their mouths wide open in shock and horror.

I held my hands up so they could see my arms. "Do you see my face?" I wailed. "See my arms? My hands?"

They both gasped. Mom grabbed Dad's arm.

"Now do you believe me?" I cried. "Now do you believe that the INSTA-TAN lotion makes hair grow?"

I stood staring at them, my chest heaving, panting loudly, tears in my eyes. I stood waiting, waiting for them to say something.

Finally, Mom broke the silence. "Larry, it isn't

the tanning lotion," she said softly, holding tightly onto Dad. "We tried to keep it from you. But we can't any longer."

"Huh? Keep *what* from me?" I demanded.

They exchanged glances. Mom let out a sob. Dad slipped his arm around her.

"It isn't the tanning lotion," Dad said in a trembling voice. "Larry, you have to know the truth now. You're growing all that hair because you're not a human. You're a dog."

## 26

I bent down and lapped up some water from the plastic water bowl Mom and Dad put on the front stoop for me. It's so hard to drink without splashing water all over my snout.

Then I bounded down the steps on all fours and joined Lily over by the evergreen shrubs. We sniffed the shrubs for a while. Then we loped off to the next yard to see if there was anything interesting to sniff.

It's been two weeks since my human body vanished and I turned back into my real dog identity. Luckily, before I changed back, Mom and Dad — or, I should say, Mr. and Mrs. Boyd — were nice enough to explain to me what had happened.

They work for Dr. Murkin, you see. In fact, everyone in town works for Dr. Murkin. The whole town is kind of an experimental testing lab.

A few years ago, Dr. Murkin found a way to change dogs into children. He discovered a serum that made us dogs look and think and act like people. That's what my shots were. He gave me fresh serum every two weeks.

But after a while, the serum doesn't work anymore. It wears off. And the children go back to being dogs.

"Dr. Murkin has decided to stop testing the serum on dogs," Mom told me. "It just doesn't work. And it causes the families too much pain when the children turn back into dogs."

"He's never going to work with dogs again," Dad explained. "The serum just doesn't last long enough with dogs. So, no more dogs."

It was nice of the Boyds to explain to me what had happened. I felt so grateful, I licked their hands. Then I ran off to find Lily and show her that I was a dog, too.

Lily and I roam around together all the time. Sometimes Manny joins us. There are so many dogs roaming around in this town. I guess they all were human for a while.

I'm glad Dr. Murkin isn't using dogs for his tests anymore. Dogs should be dogs, in my humble opinion.

Lily and I found some good dirt to sniff in the neighbors' flower garden. There aren't any flowers to dig up yet. But the dirt smells really great.

Then I saw the Boyds' car roll up the driveway. They'd been gone all afternoon. I went running up eagerly to the car, wagging my tail happily.

I jumped up and barked out a greeting.

To my surprise, Mrs. Boyd was carrying a baby. A tiny baby, tightly wrapped in pink blankets.

She held the baby in both arms, and carried it carefully up the walk toward the house. Mr. Boyd had a big smile on his face as he caught up to her.

"What a good little girl," Mrs. Boyd cooed to the baby. "Yes, you are. You're a good little girl. Welcome to your new home, Jasper."

Huh? I thought. Isn't Jasper a funny name for a little girl?

Then I stared up at the baby and saw her bright yellow eyes.

Add *more*

# Goosebumps

to your collection . . .
A chilling preview of
what's next from
R.L. STINE

## A NIGHT IN
## TERROR TOWER

# 5

I felt a chill at the back of my neck. I stepped up to the bars and peered into the small cell.

Real people stood inside this cell, I thought. Real people held on to these bars and stared out. Sat at that little writing table. Paced back and forth in that narrow space. Waiting to meet their fate.

Swallowing hard, I glanced at my brother. I could see that he was just as horrified as I was.

"We have not reached the top of the Tower yet," Mr. Starkes announced. "Let us continue our climb."

The stone steps became steeper as we made our way up the curving stairway. I trailed my hand along the wall as I followed Eddie up to the top.

And as I climbed, I suddenly had the strangest feeling — that I had been here before. That I had followed the twisting stairs. That I had climbed to the top of this ancient tower before.

Of course, that was impossible.

Eddie and I had never been to England before in our lives.

The feeling stayed with me as our tour group crowded into the tiny chamber at the top. Had I seen this tower in a movie? Had I seen pictures of it in a magazine?

Why did it look so familiar to me?

I shook my head hard, as if trying to shake away the strange, troubling thoughts. Then I stepped up beside Eddie and gazed around the tiny room.

A small round window high above our heads allowed a wash of gloomy gray light to filter down over us. The rounded walls were bare, lined with cracks and dark stains. The ceiling was low, so low that Mr. Starkes and some of the other adults had to duck their heads.

"Perhaps you can feel the sadness in this room," Mr. Starkes said softly.

We all huddled closer to hear him better. Eddie stared up at the window, his expression solemn.

"This is the tower room where a young prince and princess were brought," Mr. Starkes continued, speaking solemnly. "It was the early fifteenth century. The prince and princess — Edward and Susannah of York — were locked in this tiny tower cell."

He waved the red pennant in a circle. We all followed it, gazing around the small, cold room. "Imagine. Two children. Grabbed away from their home. Locked away in the drab chill of this cell in the top of a tower." Mr. Starkes' voice remained just above a whisper.

I suddenly felt cold. I zipped my coat back up. Eddie had his hands shoved deep in his jeans pockets. His eyes grew wide with fear as he gazed around the tiny, dark room.

"The prince and princess weren't up here for long," Mr. Starkes continued, lowering the pennant to his side. "That night while they slept, the Lord High Executioner and his men crept up the stairs. Their orders were to smother the two children. To keep the prince and princess from ever taking the throne."

Mr. Starkes shut his eyes and bowed his head. The silence in the room seemed to grow heavy.

No one moved. No one spoke.

The only sound was the whisper of wind through the tiny window above our heads.

I shut my eyes, too. I tried to picture a boy and a girl. Frightened and alone. Trying to sleep in this cold, stone room.

The door bursts open. Strange men break in. They don't say a word. They rush to smother the boy and girl.

Right in this room.

Right where I am standing now, I thought.

I opened my eyes. Eddie was gazing at me, his expression troubled. "This is . . . really scary," he whispered.

"Yeah," I agreed. Mr. Starkes started to tell us more.

But the camera fell out of my hand. It clattered noisily on the stone floor. I bent to pick it up. "Oh, look, Eddie — the lens broke!" I cried.

"Ssshhh! I missed what Mr. Starkes said about the prince and princess!" Eddie protested.

"But my camera — !" I shook it. I don't know why. It's not like shaking it would help fix the lens.

"What did he say? Did you hear?" Eddie demanded.

I shook my head. "Sorry. I missed it."

We walked over to a low cot against the wall. A three-legged wooden stool stood beside it. The only furniture in the chamber.

Did the prince and princess sit here? I wondered.

Did they stand on the bed and try to see out the window?

What did they talk about? Did they wonder what was going to happen to them? Did they talk about the fun things they would do when they were freed? When they returned home?

It was all so sad, so horribly sad.

I stepped up to the cot and rested my hand on it. It felt hard.

Black markings on the wall caught my eye. Writing?

Had the prince or the princess left a message on the wall?

I leaned over the cot and squinted at the markings.

No. No message. Just cracks in the stone.

"Sue — come on," Eddie urged. He tugged my arm.

"Okay, okay," I replied impatiently. I ran my hand over the cot again. It felt so lumpy and hard, so uncomfortable.

I gazed up at the window. The gray light had darkened to black. Dark as night out there.

The stone walls suddenly seemed to close in on me. I felt as if I were in a dark closet, a cold, frightening closet. I imagined the walls squeezing in, choking me, smothering me.

Is that how the prince and princess felt?

Was I feeling the same fear they had known over five hundred years ago?

With a heavy sigh, I let go of the cot and turned to Eddie. "Let's get out of here," I said in a trembling voice. "This room is just too frightening, too sad."

We turned away from the cot, took a few steps toward the stairs — and stopped.

"Hey — !" We both cried out in surprise.

Mr. Starkes and the tour group had disappeared.

# 6

"Where did they go?" Eddie cried in a shrill, startled voice. "They *left* us here!"

"They must be on their way back down the stairs," I told him. I gave him a gentle push. "Let's go."

Eddie lingered close to me. "You go first," he insisted quietly.

"You're not scared — are you?" I teased. "All alone in the Terror Tower?"

I don't know why I enjoy teasing my little brother so much. I *knew* he was scared. I was a little scared, too. But I couldn't help it.

As I said, Eddie doesn't always bring out the best in me.

I led the way to the twisting stairs. As I peered down, they seemed even darker and steeper.

"Why didn't we hear them leave?" Eddie demanded. "Why did they leave so fast?"

"It's late," I told him. "I think Mr. Starkes was eager to get everyone on the bus and back to their hotels. The tower closes at five, I think." I glanced at my watch. It was five-twenty.

"Hurry," Eddie pleaded. "I don't want to be locked in. This place gives me the creeps."

"Me, too," I confessed.

Squinting into the darkness, I started down the steps. My sneakers slid on the smooth stone. Once again, I pressed one hand against the wall. It helped me keep my balance on the curving stairs.

"Where *are* they?" Eddie demanded nervously. "Why can't we hear the others on the stairs?"

The air grew cooler as we climbed lower. A pale yellow light washed over the landing just below us.

My hand swept through something soft and sticky. Cobwebs.

Yuck.

I could hear Eddie's rapid breathing behind me. "The bus will wait for us," I told him. "Just stay calm. Mr. Starkes won't drive off without us."

*"Is anybody down there?"* Eddie screamed. *"Can anybody hear me?"*

His shrill voice echoed down the narrow stone stairwell.

No reply.

"Where are the guards?" Eddie demanded.

"Eddie — please don't get worked up," I pleaded. "It's late. The guards are probably closing up. Mr. Starkes will be waiting for us down there. I promise you."

We stepped into the pale light of the landing. The small cell we had seen before stood against the wall.

"Don't stop," Eddie pleaded, breathing hard. "Keep going, Sue. Hurry!"

I put my hand on his shoulder to calm him. "Eddie, we'll be fine," I said soothingly. "We're almost down to the ground."

"But, look — " Eddie protested. He pointed frantically.

I saw at once what was troubling him. There were *two* stairways leading down — one to the left of the cell, and one to the right.

"That's strange," I uttered, glancing from one to the other. "I don't remember a second stairway."

"Wh-which one is the right one?" he stammered.

I hesitated. "I'm not sure," I replied. I stepped over to the one on the right and peered down. I couldn't see very far because it curved so sharply.

"Which one? Which one?" Eddie repeated.

"I don't think it matters," I told him. "I mean, they both lead *down* — right?"

I motioned for him to follow me. "Come on. I think this is the one we took when we were climbing up."

I took one step down.

Then stopped.

I heard footsteps. Heavy footsteps. Coming *up* the stairs.

Eddie grabbed my hand. "Who's that?" he whispered.

"Probably Mr. Starkes," I told him. "He must be coming back up to get us."

Eddie breathed a long sigh of relief.

"Mr. Starkes — is that you?" I called down.

Silence. Except for the approaching footsteps.

"Mr. Starkes?" I called in a tiny voice.

When the dark figure appeared on the stairway below, I could see at once that it wasn't our tour guide.

"Oh!" I uttered a startled cry as the huge man in the black cape stepped into view.

His face was still hidden in darkness. But his eyes glowed like burning coals as he glared up at Eddie and me from under the black, wide-brimmed hat.

"Is — is this the way down?" I stammered.

He didn't reply.

He didn't move. His eyes burned into mine.

I struggled to see his face. But he kept it hidden in the shadow of the hat, pulled low over his forehead.

I took a deep breath and tried again. "We got separated from our group," I said. "They must be waiting for us. Is — is this the way down?"

Again, he didn't reply. He glared up at us menacingly.

He's so big, I realized. He blocks the entire stairway.

"Sir — ?" I started. "My brother and I — "

He raised a hand. A huge hand, covered in a black glove.

He pointed up at us.

"You will come with me now," he growled.

I just stared at him. I didn't understand.

"You will come now," he repeated. "I do not want to hurt you. But if you try to escape, I will have no choice."

# About the Author

R.L. STINE is the author of over three dozen bestselling thrillers and mysteries for young people. Recent titles for teenagers include *I Saw You That Night!*, *Call Waiting*, *Halloween Night II*, *The Dead Girlfriend*, and *The Baby-sitter III*, all published by Scholastic. He is also the author of the *Fear Street* series.

Bob lives in New York City with his wife, Jane, and fourteen-year-old son, Matt.

# Goosebumps™

Sue and Eddie are having a blast visiting old castles in London...until they get separated from their tour group.

There's no way their guide would just leave them. All alone. In a gloomy old tower. There's no way they'd get locked inside. After dark. With those eerie sounds. With a strange, creepy dark figure.

There's no way out in...

# A NIGHT IN TERROR TOWER

## Goosebumps #27
## by R.L. STINE

*Terrorizing a bookstore near you!*

# GET Goosebumps
## by R.L. Stine

☐ BAB47745-5 **#23 Return of the Mummy** $3.50

☐ BAB48354-4 **#24 Phantom of the Auditorium** $3.50

☐ BAB48355-2 **#25 Attack of the Mutant** $3.50

☐ BAB48350-1 **#26 My Hairiest Adventure** $3.50

☐ BAB48351-X **#27 A Night in Terror Tower** $3.50

☐ BAB48352-8 **#28 The Cuckoo Clock of Doom** $3.50

☐ BAB48347-1 **#29 Monster Blood III** $3.50

☐ BAB48348-X **#30 It Came from Beneath the Sink** $3.50

☐ BAB48349-8 **#31 The Night of the Living Dummy II** $3.50

☐ BAB48344-7 **#32 The Barking Ghost** $3.50

☐ BAB48345-5 **#33 The Horror at Camp Jellyjam** $3.50

☐ BAB48346-3 **#34 Revenge of the Lawn Gnomes** $3.50

☐ BAB48340-4 **#35 A Shocker on Shock Street** $3.50

☐ BAB56873-6 **#36 The Haunted Mask II** $3.50

☐ BAB56874-4 **#37 The Headless Ghost** $3.50

☐ BAB56875-2 **#38 The Abominable Snowman
of Pasadena** $3.50

------------------------------------------------------------

### Scare me, thrill me, mail me GOOSEBUMPS Now!

Available wherever you buy books, or use this order form. Scholastic Inc., P.O. Box 7502,
2931 East McCarty Street, Jefferson City, MO 65102

Please send me the books I have checked above. I am enclosing $_____ (please add
$2.00 to cover shipping and handling). Send check or money order — no cash or C.O.D.s please.

Name _____ Age _____

Address _____

City _____ State/Zip _____

Please allow four to six weeks for delivery. Offer good in the U.S. only. Sorry, mail orders are not available to
residents of Canada. Prices subject to change.

GB53095